Big & Bad

IRELAND LORELEI

Contents

Note to Readers

The characters in this book are unapologetic and dramatic. The scenes are steamy, and the road to happily ever after maybe twisted. This book is meant for audiences 18 years old and older. Triggering events include profanity, sex, violence, death among other things.

Prologue

IVY

I VY BALDWIN, THAT'S ME, a name I've striven to etch in the grand tapestry of the fashion world. I've always felt destined for this path, a journey that's taken me from the radiant shores of my hometown of Huntsville, AL, to the bustling streets of Manhattan.

Becoming a fashion model wasn't just an aspiration; it felt more like an undeniable calling. With my striking features and a presence that commanded attention, my journey in the realm of high fashion was destined to be nothing short of extraordinary. It began humbly, gracing local runways and participating in modest photoshoots, but my undeniable charisma and innate talent soon captured the eyes of prestigious modeling agencies. Fashion shows from New York to London have given me so much exposure.

London, a city brimming with history and at the forefront of cutting-edge fashion, became the stage where my life took a thrilling turn. It was amidst the grandeur of iconic landmarks and the electric energy of the fashion world that I was introduced to the enigmatic world of

BDSM. This transformative moment in my life was ignited during a high-profile photoshoot in the heart of London. While the camera's lens captured me in exquisite garments, the real focus was on the intense chemistry between me and a mysterious and charismatic Dom, Paul. Our connection was magnetic, awakening my curiosity about the world of BDSM.

Intrigued by the allure of submission and dominance, I began to delve deeper into this clandestine lifestyle. Behind the glamorous facade of my modeling career, I embraced the exhilarating experiences of power dynamics and intimate exploration. The lines between my life on the runway and my secret life as a submissive started to blur, adding a layer of complexity to my persona. It led me into the turbulent waters of emotions. I found myself falling deeply in love with my Dom, an emotion I believed to be the most profound connection I had ever experienced. But my Dom, unwavering in his commitment to a loveless, purely BDSM relationship, refused to reciprocate. The resulting emotional chasm threatened to shatter the beautiful world we had constructed together.

The end of my contract with my first Dom marked a crossroads in my life. I emerged from the experience with a wounded heart, and I vowed never to let love and emotions intertwine with my next partner. The pain of unrequited love served as a poignant reminder of the fine line between passion and heartache, a line I was determined never to cross again. Now, I stand on the threshold of a new beginning, seeking a new Dom who can ignite the flames of my desires without kindling the flames and safeguarding my heart.

A year later...

Melody Remington, my best friend and famous actress, went to The Fourth Base Dungeon without me two years ago and found the loves of her life in this club. I couldn't believe it. She not only couldn't choose between them, but didn't have to. They chose her, and they live together as happily as I have ever seen her. And as for me, I can't find one Dom that wants to blur the lines and fall in love with me.

Now every time I am in the city, it is the place to be. I have experienced some scenes at parties, but have not signed any new contracts since Paul. But every time I step into The Dungeon, the air practically hums with energy, a mix of sensual tension and raw power. Dim lighting cast flickering shadows over the plush leather furniture, and the soft sounds of conversation were punctuated by the occasional crack of a whip from one of the private rooms. The scent of expensive whiskey, leather, and something unmistakably decadent filled the space. I had traveled the world, walked the most exclusive runways, and attended the most luxurious parties, but this? This is intoxicating. It was exactly the kind of temptation I desperately needed, but also somewhat avoided.

Tonight is no different, as I take in the submissives kneeling at their Dom's feet, the way power and control flow between partners like an unspoken language. My stomach tightened, my body remembering what it was like to surrender to that kind of intensity. I have been trying to convince myself that I didn't need this world anymore. I have tried to leave it behind after Paul broke my heart, telling myself that this really wasn't for me. But standing here now, feeling the pulse of dominance and submission around me, I knew the truth. I missed it. I missed the rush, the surrender, and the feeling of being completely consumed.

That's when he walked up, Noah Ferguson, with Brody. I didn't need an introduction to know who he was. I had heard his name whispered between Melody's men before, always with a hint of respect and maybe even a little fear. Noah was the owner of Elite Security. The one who made sure every event, every club, and every high-profile client in The Society stayed protected.

The first thing I noticed about him was his size. He was big. Tall, broad-shouldered, and built like a man who knew how to handle himself. His dark skin, deep eyes, and bold head were a turn-on for me. His jaw was sharp enough to cut glass.

He glanced my way, and the look in his eyes got me. They were cold, assessing, like he had already decided I wasn't worth his time before I even said a word. I was used to being admired, even worshipped. I had spent years in front of cameras, walking runways, and gracing magazine covers. Men fawned over me, and Doms wanted to claim me. But Noah? He looked at me like I was something stuck to the bottom of his boot.

Brody, Chaz, and Jaxon greeted him like old friends. Melody told him hello, but when Brody gestured between us and said, "Noah, this is Ivy," I swear the man barely acknowledged me.

"Yeah. I know who she is."

His voice was deep, rough, but it was the dismissiveness in his tone that made my spine stiffen.

I arched a brow. "And yet, I don't think I know you."

His eyes flicked over me, unimpressed. "That's probably for the best."

Melody tensed beside me, but I didn't need her to step in. I had dealt with men like him before, men who thought they had me figured out before I even opened my mouth.

"Oh? And why is that?" I asked, tilting my head, my voice all honey and silk.

Noah didn't so much as blink. "Because I don't waste my time on spoiled little celebrities who feel like every man should fall and worship at their feet. No pun intended, Melody. You don't wear you're fame on you like a medal or something."

His words were precise, sharp, meant to sting. And maybe they would have if I weren't so damn intrigued.

Instead, I smiled. A slow, deliberate curve of my lips. Oh, he was going to be fun to mess with.

"Good thing I don't waste my time on men who make assumptions before they actually know someone," I countered smoothly. "Aren't you just charming?"

Melody snorts in the background, but I don't look away.

"Just real," he answers.

"And here I thought Doms were supposed to be polite."

He steps closer. "I'm not your Dom. I don't play with tourists, especially the kind who think this lifestyle is just another stage to perform on."

"Good. I'm not a tourist." I reply not in an angry tone, but in a firm one.

"No? You sure you know the difference between pain and foreplay?"

"I do. Do you know the difference between being a Dom and just being an asshole?"

Chaz and Brody smirked. Jaxon looked like he was watching a live chess match. And Melody? She was grinning like she had just won the lottery. But Noah? He just stared at me for a long moment, with those cold, assessing eyes giving away nothing. Then, without another word, he turned on his heel and walked away. I watched him go, a flicker of something unfamiliar twisting in my stomach. Oh, I definitely wasn't done with Mr. Noah Ferguson.

Melody leaned in, her voice practically vibrating with excitement. "Oh, honey. You like him."

"I do not," I scoffed. "I just enjoy proving men like him wrong."

Brody chuckled. "That's going to be fun to watch." Chaz and Jaxon nodded and laughed.

I lifted my glass of champagne to my lips, letting the bubbles tickle my throat as I kept my gaze locked on Noah's retreating form. He thought he had me figured out. Thought I was some shallow, spoiled model who didn't belong in his world. He had no idea. But he would. But in three days, I have to head back out to Paris for a two-week-long photo shoot. But when I get back, he will get to see the real me, I will make sure of it.

Noah

The night begins like any other. It's barely nine, and already, The Fourth Base Dungeon is humming with energy. The velvet-dark shadows, crimson lighting, and the low hum of bass that pulses through the floor like a second heartbeat. I walk the perimeter, silent, invisible. My eyes scan the room, each face. It's all muscle memory by now. I've been doing this long enough to know when something feels off before it even happens. A flicker of hesitation in a submissive's step. A Dom with too much edge in his voice. An unfamiliar face that doesn't belong. And so far? Everything's clean.

The club looks like seduction and smells like control. You can smell the cologne, leather, desire, and fear. It's exactly how I like it.

My name is Noah Ferguson, and I own Elite Security. Every inch of this place is under my protection. My company handles the security here, The Spice Club, and every single high-profile event The Society throws. I mainly work here at The Dungeon, but I occasionally check in at The Spice Club and work the special events. I don't babysit. I don't do emotions. You want safe, discreet, brutal efficiency? You call my company. I hire the best of the best, mostly retired military. Some are in the lifestyle and some are not, but all are discreet and professional.

I move past a couple pressed against the edge of the bar, the Dom whispering something into his submissive's ear that makes her shiver. She's on her knees five seconds later, perfectly obedient. I nod once, approving. That's how it's supposed to look. Not messy. Not chaotic but controlled, consensual, and clean.

When I reach the private lounge, I find Brody leaning against the wall like he owns the place, which, technically, he does: he and his best friends. Chaz is nearby, talking to one of the Dungeon servers, and Jaxon's lounging with Melody, their girl, curled up on his lap like she was born to be there.

Brody glances up and gives me that smirk that says he's about to cause trouble. "Noah."

"Brody."

"How does everything look out there tonight?"

"This place is full, but everything is going smoothly. No issues or problems. I have the normal crew here tonight. Joey is at the door, Dion and Bryan are roaming, Tray is on the cameras in the security room, and Maggie is outside the hallway door to the private rooms."

He chuckles. "Glad to see the normal crew is all back together. Dion was missed while on vacation, not that Vince was bad, but the normal crew just flows together." He pushes off the wall. "Come, meet someone. I think you will like her, and she needs a new Dom."

"No thanks." I already know where this is going.

He ignores me, of course. Bastard always does.

"She's Melody's best friend," he says as he walks toward the corner of the lounge. "Been out of the scene for a while. Heard she's looking for a new Dom."

This is the part I hate. I love these guys like brothers, but I am not looking for a new sub right now. And especially tonight. Tonight, I am on duty. I'm here to protect. To control the chaos. To keep people safe. I follow him anyway because if Melody's best friend, Ivy Baldwin, is here, I need the team to be alerted. The people who come to The Dungeon are members of the society and respect each other's privacy. I mean, they are all rich by one means or another, but sometimes visitors don't have that same "not caught up in the fan" mode.

And yea, there she is, Ivy Baldwin. She looks like fire. Long, dark hair cascading over her shoulders like silk. Skin like caramel cream and legs for days. Her outfit is subtle and classy, but her eyes, God help me, her eyes are anything but subtle. Green, sharp, intelligent. Like she's daring me to underestimate her.

Brody gestures between us. "Noah, this is Ivy."

"Yeah. I know who she is."

She arched a brow. "And yet, I don't think I know you."

I am unimpressed. "That's probably for the best."

"Oh? And why is that?" she asked.

"Because I don't waste my time on spoiled little celebrities who feel like every man should fall and worship at their feet. No pun intended, Melody. You don't wear you're fame on you like a medal or something."

"Good thing I don't waste my time on men who make assumptions before they actually know someone," she countered smoothly. "Aren't you just charming?"

Melody snorts in the background, but Ivy doesn't look away. She studies me with those cutting eyes.

"Just real," I answer.

Her lips twitch. A smirk. Almost a smile. "And here I thought Doms were supposed to be polite."

I step closer. "I'm not your Dom."

That does it. The smile fades. Something flashes in her gaze, hurt? Surprise? Maybe curiosity. Whatever it is, I shut it down fast.

"I don't play with tourists," I say. "Especially the kind who think this lifestyle is just another stage to perform on."

I see her flinch at that. Barely. But it's there.

Brody shoots me a glare, but I ignore him.

Ivy lifts her chin. "Good. I'm not a tourist."

"No?" I tilt my head. "You sure you know the difference between pain and foreplay?"

"I do," she says, cool and clear. "Do you know the difference between being a Dom and just being an asshole?"

Chaz chokes on his drink behind me, and Jaxon laughs outright.

But I'm not laughing. Because for the first time in a long damn while... someone just called me out. And I felt it. More than I should have.

Chapter One
Giving In

MELODY

C HAZ IS LEANING AGAINST the marble island, sipping from a tumbler of ginger whiskey, muscles coiled in that relaxed way that makes women trip over themselves in his presence. I know better. I know what lives under that calm—the storm, the heat, the devotion.

I step into his space, tugging the glass from his hand and taking a sip.

"Mel?" he asks, eyes narrowing with curiosity.

"I need a favor."

He waits.

"It's Ivy. She's leaving for Paris in the morning. She's been holding herself too tight for too long. She's craving submission, but she won't admit it. She needs to feel it again. Not just remember it, to feel it."

Chaz's jaw ticks once. "And what does that have to do with me?"

"Would you please do a scene with her tonight? I know it is unorthodox, me loaning one of my lovers and Doms out, but she is my best friend, and she is drowning, and I have to help her get her head above the water."

"So, you are asking me to do a scene with her? Why not one of the other guys?"

"Because what you give to a woman in dominance is exactly what she needs. Please? No sex. You know I don't share with anyone like that! But, just a scene, in public, totally controlled at The Dungeon. She needs to feel safe... and exposed."

He considers me quietly, then nods once. "Okay. But only because you asked. And what do I get for doing this favor?"

"Anything you want, Daddy!"

"I will let you know when I am going to take what I want as payment, my little Pet!"

I knew when I decided to ask that my Dom would make sure he got something out of the deal. But that's okay with me! I know that he understands what I'm really asking him to do, and that is to remind her of who she is, a sub.

Ivy

It's my last night in town before Paris, and I should be packing. Or sleeping. Or doing something productive. Instead, I'm pacing Melody's living room, trying to avoid the knowing look she keeps throwing me from the couch. All I can think of is Noah, that arrogant asshole.

"Ivy," she says finally, her voice velvet with a steel core beneath it, "you need a scene."

I pause mid-step, turn toward her, and cross my arms. "I need about eight hours of sleep and a vacation."

She cocks her head. "Well, I agree with the vacation. You know, I didn't think you should take this shoot. You are so tired. But you need to give in to your desires. I know you miss being a sub and giving up control. You miss the bondage, the dominance, the pain; you miss it all, and not having it is like not having caffeine! You are irritable and miserable."

I sigh. "Mel—"

"You're going to another continent to drape yourself in couture and charm a thousand photographers, but you haven't let go in months. You did that one scene months ago in Europe. But you and I both know it was short and just to give you enough to satisfy your craving. You need more. Just because Paul is a dick doesn't mean you walk away from the lifestyle. It just means that he wasn't the one who deserved your submission and your heart."

I roll my eyes. "I know. It is just hard to think about getting back into another contract with someone. How do I hold my heart out of it? I know there are subs that do, but I am not one of them who can keep my emotions out of it. And honestly, I'm fine."

"You're not," she says gently, standing and walking over to me. "Ivy, you're spinning. You're pushing down everything. You're craving to give up control. You need to remember what it feels like to surrender. To be seen."

My throat tightens. I want to argue, but I don't. Because she's right.

She wraps her fingers around mine. "Let it go. Just for tonight. Trust me."

I swallow, quietly.

Melody presses a kiss to my cheek. "I already asked Chaz."

I blink. "You what?"

"He said yes."

Before I can argue, she's gone, walking off down the hall toward the kitchen like she didn't just lob a grenade into my evening.

Ivy

That night...

The Dungeon is pulsing with energy when we arrive. It always hits me in the chest the moment I walk in. I have always loved the hum of leather, the scent of arousal, and hearing the moans drifting from shadowed corners.

Chaz is already waiting near the center stage when Melody leads me through the crowd. He's dressed in a black, tailored, fitted tux. No wonder, Mel had me where this expensive gown tonight. It is for the scene. He stands there commanding without even trying. His expression is unreadable, but there's something in his eyes when he sees me, something like patience or maybe even understanding.

"Ivy." His voice is deep, calm, and steady.

I swallow hard. "Chaz."

"Melody explained what you need. If you want out at any time, say 'pearl.' That's your safe word."

I nod.

"Are you sure?" he asks. "You have to choose this."

I don't answer right away. I take a breath, the kind that scrapes the edges of old wounds on its way out. And then I nod again.

"Yes. I choose this."

He holds out his hand.

I take it.

The Dungeon grows quiet as we ascend the stage. All eyes are on us. In this world, scenes are sacred. They're honored. And I know Chaz will protect me from everything except what I need to face.

The scene starts off slow. With a mellow, slow dance music playing overhead. He pulls me close and we start to dance. When the song ends, he steps back with a look in his eyes that I have seen so many times with other Doms, pure dominance and control.

"Strip," he says loud enough for everyone in the room to hear.

My heart slams with excitement that has been built up for months. I can feel everyone in the place has stopped and is watching us. I obey.

Slowly, I slide the dress down my body, letting it pool at my feet. I'm wearing nothing beneath it but black lace panties. My skin prickles with exposure, the attention settling on me like a weighted cloak.

Chaz steps behind me. "Hands behind your back."

I obey.

He binds my wrists with black silk, firm but gentle. His fingers brush against my pulse, steadying me.

"You are not here to please them," he murmurs. "You are here to remember you."

Then he moves like a shadow and storm, commanding the space without ever raising his voice. He uses a crop, flicking it lightly against my inner thighs, then the base of my spine. He circles me, slow and deliberate, never striking hard, but enough to wake up nerves I forgot I had.

My breath catches. My knees weaken. But I don't fall.

"Beautiful," he says. "So, fucking beautiful like this."

He brings out the rope next. Smooth, soft, and cool against my skin. His touch isn't hesitant, but it's not rushed either. He knows exactly what he's doing, and my body responds before my brain has the chance to analyze it. I focus on his hands as they move the rope across my skin, looping it around my torso and upper arms, crossing between my breasts, wrapping and weaving until I feel the shift in pressure.

"This is what surrender looks like," he says, voice carrying. "Not weakness. Not fragility, but power."

The harness doesn't just bind. It holds. I tremble, not from pain, but from release. Tears burn at the corners of my eyes. Not because I'm sad. Because for the first time in months, I feel free. My breathing changes, deeper now, fuller. Each inhale tightens the embrace of the rope, reminding me that I've given up control and I am loving it.

"Breathe into it," Chaz murmurs from behind me, close to my ear. "Let your body feel what it's been missing."

I do, and it nearly unravels me. The silence in the Dungeon is deafening. No one speaks.

He steps in front of me, and I lift my eyes to his without needing to be told. I expect intensity. What I find is reverence.

"You're stunning like this," he says softly. "But it's not the rope. It's not the stage. It's you. You, finally letting go."

I swallow hard. My throat feels too tight. My skin feels too alive.

"Turn," he commands.

I pivot on trembling legs, the silk of the rope shifting slightly with the movement. He runs a hand down my spine, and every inch of me lights up like a fuse. He adds a soft black blindfold over my eyes, and the world disappears. I have to just feel his presence and every touch.

The sting of a crop comes next, not too hard, but just enough to make me moan out in pain. My breath hitches on the first strike against the back of my thigh. I let out a soft, involuntary moan. My knees threaten to buckle. He presses a hand to my lower back to stabilize me before another strike on the other thigh. Another flick just under the curve of my ass. I flinch at the pain that feels so good.

"Good girl," Chaz praises, voice like warm smoke curling through my spine. "Take it. You're doing beautifully."

Then he flicks the crop harder and more frequently from the backs of my thighs to my ass, to my stomach, my nipples, and then between my thighs, hitting that sensitive spot that makes me moan out in pleasure and pain. He continues for what seems like hours, but yet seems too short. I have missed this. I miss the pain, the surrender, the pleasure it brings to my body. I needed this so much, even if I didn't want to admit it.

Noah

As I was making my rounds tonight, the crowd got quiet. I turned towards the center stage, not expecting to see Ivy and Chaz getting ready for a scene. But when I notice it is her, every fucking part of me pays attention. She is dressed in a skintight, red gown that must have cost a fortune. The lights dim except for the stage itself, and soft romantic music starts to play. Chaz holds out his hand, and when she takes it, he pulls her close. They dance seductively to the music until the song ends. Once it does, Chaz takes a step back and says, "Strip," so we could all hear him.

When she lets that red dress drop to the floor, her tits bounce and they are absolutely beautiful and perky, just waiting for someone to nibble on them. She stands there in nothing but a pair of black silk panties. At first, I tell myself I'm watching because I'm curious, curious how a model used to command runways and camera lenses can navigate a world where she is the one being commanded.

Her shoulders settle. Her breath is deep, even, and her body is relaxed. There's no camera on her, no fashion week fanfare, no lighting crew. Just her half-naked in front of the entire room, and giving up control. And somehow more powerful than I've ever seen her.

Chaz handles her with precision and care, and I watch the way her body responds to each strike, each touch, each word.

My instincts won't shut up though, because submission in a scene is one thing. It's a moment in time. But outside of that? In a structured contract? In the quiet, messy hours between? That's different. And I don't know if Ivy Baldwin, the supermodel whose face is plastered on billboards and who commands entire rooms without speaking, can let go without being in the public scenes where she is judged for her submissiveness.

However, it is her in the scene that I know I will not be able to get out of my mind.

Chapter Two
Taken

Ivy

T HE MOMENT THE WHEELS screech against the tarmac, a sharp jolt vibrates through the cabin and jars me from the shallow sleep I'd finally managed to drift into somewhere over the Atlantic. Paris to New York, then connecting home. It's glamorous on paper and hell in reality. My neck aches, my spine feels like it's been wrung out, and my feet, still trapped in heels meant more for photos than function, are throbbing in line with every heartbeat.

As the jet taxis toward the gate, all I can think about is Melody, sushi, cocktails, laughter, and one step closer to giving Noah Ferguson a run for his money.

Melody had begged me not to take the Paris show. She told me I'd been overworking myself. She wasn't wrong. But the bookings were too good, the designers too legendary, the exposure too priceless. Still, as I scroll through my messages and see her name lighting up the screen, a smile tugs at my lips.

Melody:

> *Get your fine ass home. Jaxon's cooking steaks on the grill. We're waiting.*

God, I've missed her. I've missed them all, but I am a little nervous about seeing Chaz again. I mean, the last time I saw him, he was dominating me at The Dungeon. I just hope things are not weird between us, including Mel.

As I step into the airport, it is mostly empty. I keep my head down, wheeling my Louis Vuitton behind me, nodding politely to a few people who glance too long. Customs is a breeze, and within half an hour, I'm stepping through the glass doors and into the heavy warmth of the night. My phone buzzes again.

Melody:

> **You want us to pick you up?**

I laugh under my breath, thumbs already flying.
Me:

> *I've got it. I'm not helpless. I'm tired and hungry, but not helpless.*

I scan the curb. No sign of my car yet, and the ride-share app is stuck in loading purgatory. I sigh. Just then, a car glides up to the curb with a little too much ease. The man driving it steps out with robotic precision and opens the back door with a practiced smile.

"Ms. Baldwin?"

I pause mid-step. "Yes?"

"Uber service. Miss Remington arranged it."

That sounds like her, always erring on the side of caution since her world became tied to three possessive Doms and their nearly militant sense of protection. Honestly, it tracks. I glance at my phone again. No confirmation from her. No sudden texts. Still, maybe it slipped her mind.

He gestures toward the open door. "Flat rate. Already covered."

The seats are black leather. The inside smells like cologne and lemon polish. Cold air whispers from the vents. I'm tired. Bone-deep, muscle-numb tired. I slide inside. The door shuts with a finality that feels... wrong.

I turn slightly, placing my bag beside me, and watch as the driver gets in and pulls away from the curb with unnatural smoothness. My hand instinctively brushes over my phone. I unlock it, glance again for a message from Melody. Nothing.

"You live around here?" the driver asks, not bothering to look at me.

I blink. "I'm sorry?"

"You travel a lot," he says, eyes on the road. "Saw you in that Paris show. You wore that blue silk number with the feathers. Big hit."

A slow, cold dread begins to settle in my stomach. That wasn't on TV. That wasn't public. Only people in the room or with serious access would know about that.

I adjust in my seat, tensing. "You follow fashion that closely?"

He doesn't answer. Just turns off the main road onto a side street I don't recognize. There are no lights. No cars. Just empty space and shadows.

My heart skips. "Excuse me, you missed the main turn. The freeway is—"

"We're taking a quicker way," he replies flatly.

No. No, we're not. I straighten. "I'm not comfortable with this. Pull over. I'll call a different car."

The locks engage again. This time, audibly. Intentionally. I press the button on the door. Nothing. The windows tint themselves automatically. Blacked out. The divider that had been subtle now becomes obvious, a one-way glass mirror.

He doesn't say another word. I reach for my phone. Dead. No signal. And now I know. I'm not being paranoid. I'm being taken. I try to keep calm, breathing in through my nose and out through my mouth, just like Paul used to teach me when we played in scenes too intense for casual spaces. Keep your head. Don't show fear. Use your mind.

Still, I speak clearly. "I have people who will know I'm missing. They will hunt you down. You know that, right?"

He doesn't even blink. "I was just told to grab you. That's it."

"By whom?"

No answer. Of course not.

The buildings start to thin out. We're moving into an industrial zone now, warehouse after warehouse, abandoned-looking, with broken windows and faded signage.

The car stops abruptly. He climbs out. When he opens the door, I lunge, but he's prepared. A prick at my neck. It is cold, fast, and something numbing. I fall back, my limbs suddenly heavy, like I'm underwater. I am conscious and aware, but slowly everything goes dark.

When I open my eyes again, I feel groggy. I have no idea how long I have been out. I blink my eyes a few times to try and focus. When I am finally able to see clearly, I notice that my bag and my phone are nowhere in sight. Whoever paid that taxi driver to pick me up and bring me here, I don't see them. My heart is pounding so hard I can feel it in my ears. Who would do this to me? And what do they want? How long will it take for Melody to realize I am missing, and how long will it take for someone to find me?

The room is nothing more than concrete and shadows. Cold, damp, and industrial in the worst kind of way. The walls are unpainted cinder block, water-stained and chipped in places, like they've been holding in secrets for far too long. The air is stale, thick with the scent of mold, dust, and oil like a mechanic's shop that hasn't seen daylight in years. There's a low mechanical hum in the background, constant and unsettling, like an old generator fighting to stay alive.

I'm seated in the center of it all, under a single bare bulb that swings gently above me, casting nauseating shadows that dance across the floor every time it moves. The floor beneath my feet is hard and uneven. I can feel the cracks in the concrete through my heels. My ankles are zip-tied to the legs of the chair, my wrists bound behind my back, digging into the skin just enough to be painful but not enough to draw blood. I take in everything, the door, the light, and even the crates stacked against the back wall. A rusted tool cart that looks like it hasn't been touched in years. There's a single steel table by the far wall, with what looks like a few random items on top of it. I can't see clearly from here what they are.

The door groans on its hinges and creaks open again, the sound dragging painfully through the still air. He walks in like he's on a coffee break. He is relaxed, indifferent, like this is just another Tuesday for him. He sets a plastic container and a water bottle down on a metal crate beside me, not looking directly at me. His body language is calculated nonchalance.

"You're going to sit tight," he mutters, adjusting the strap of the shoulder holster beneath his jacket. "This ain't personal."

"Bullshit," I say without hesitation, my voice sharp despite the dryness in my throat. "You said that you were hired, and that makes it very personal."

He glances at me, the corner of his mouth twitching.

"You talk too much," he says flatly.

I smile slowly. "I haven't even started."

He shifts, folding his arms. I notice the way his stance widens slightly, defensive.

"You got any idea who I am?" I ask, cocking my head as much as I can in the restraints. "You think I'm just some pretty face on a runway? That I cry over broken nails and designer delays?"

He doesn't even blink an eye.

I am trying to be brave and show that I am not scared, even though I am terrified. I hope he doesn't see it. "I've had agents tell me I'd never make it. I've had my heart shattered by someone I trusted with everything." My voice lowers, tightens. "You think a zip tie and a warehouse are going to scare me?"

That gets a reaction. "Careful," he says, walking slowly toward the table against the far wall. "You keep talking like that, you might make me like you."

The thought makes bile rise in my throat. "You don't get to like me. You don't get to pretend this is normal. You're a coward, playing lapdog to someone too afraid to come at me face-to-face."

He pauses. That one hit.

"You should worry less about me," he finally says, not turning around, "and more about who paid for you."

People in the industry who hated my rising star. Men, I turned down on camera and off. Bitter exes. Jealous rivals. Threats I never took seriously because I didn't think they could reach me. Not behind the lights and the lenses. Not with security teams, press agents, and layers of fame protecting me.

He moves back to the door, pulling out his phone. His voice is low when he speaks, too low for me to hear, but his posture has changed. He's on edge, tensed, even like something's gone wrong. He walks out the door and locks it from the outside.

God, I hope Melody's guys are already tracking me.

Chapter Three
Worried About Her Best Friend

MELODY

I GLANCE AT THE clock again, 10:34 PM. She should be here by now; it's been hours since I got a text from her. That is plenty of time for her to go home, unpack, shower, and get here. I press my lips together, trying to stay calm as I pace the living room of our beachside house, phone in hand. The wind outside rattles the tall windows, and somewhere in the kitchen, I hear Jaxon's deep voice teasing Brody about burning the rice. The smell of ginger and garlic wafts through the air. Everything feels normal. But it's not, because Ivy isn't here yet, and she is never late. Not without calling. I lower myself onto the edge of the couch, pulling my phone closer as I check my messages again. Still nothing. I tap the screen, pull up our text thread, and start typing another message.

Me:

I wait for five minutes, and there is nothing. No read receipt. No typing bubbles. I tap her name and hit the call button. It rings and rings until the voicemail picks up. I hang up without leaving a message and call again. It goes to her voicemail again. My chest tightens.

"Okay," I whisper, more to myself than anything. "Okay. She's probably just tired. Fell asleep after a shower or maybe she got stuck in traffic, or maybe her phone died..."

I'm already shaking my head as I say it. Because Ivy? She doesn't just disappear. She's always plugged in, always aware. She may pretend she's careless and flippant, but I know better. She's careful and smart. Something isn't right, I know it. I can feel it. I tap out another message.

Me:

> If you're ghosting me, I swear I'll hack your IG and post your worst runway shots. If this has anything to do with you being embarrassed about your scene with Chaz, we are all good here. ANSWER ME.

Still nothing. My anxiety curdles into full-on panic. I open a browser window and search for her flight number. It takes a few clicks to find the arrival board. Flight 4436 from Paris via New York. Delta.

Status: Arrived – On Time – 8:17 PM.

I freeze. She landed nearly two hours ago.

I immediately press the number for the airport.

It rings three times before a woman answers. "Greenwich International, operations desk, this is Dana."

"Hi, yes. I'm trying to confirm if a passenger on Flight 4436 deboarded. Her name is Ivy Baldwin."

"I'm sorry, we can't release individual passenger data—"

"I know," I say quickly, pressing a palm to my forehead. "I'm not trying to breach privacy laws. I'm just, she's my best friend; she was supposed to meet me. She landed over an hour ago, and I haven't heard from her. I've called and texted, and I just need to know if she got off the plane. I am getting worried about her."

There's a pause. Typing. "That flight landed on time. 8:17 PM, gate C6. All passengers cleared customs. No reported incidents."

"Are you sure?"

"Yes, ma'am."

I close my eyes. "Okay. Thank you."

I hang up and immediately pull up Ivy's location on Find My Friends. Nothing. Not shared. We always share our locations with each other when we are out of town, out of the country, whether I am on a movie set or she is at a photo shoot.

"Mel?" Jaxon's voice cuts through the spiral. He's standing in the doorway, still wearing his apron, his brows pulled together. "What's wrong?"

I don't answer right away. I just hold up my phone. "Ivy's flight landed at 8:17. She isn't here yet. She's not answering. Her location isn't shared. It isn't like her. I am worried."

Chaz appears behind him, towel slung over his shoulder. "What do you mean she's not answering? That's not like her."

"I know it's not like her." I jump up, pacing again. My heart is hammering in my chest. "She always texts when she lands. She always checks in. And the airport said everyone got off the flight just fine, so unless she slipped past customs like a damn ninja, she was there. Something happened. I know it."

Brody enters last, quiet, serious. He walks straight over and takes the phone from my hand, looking at the screen before placing a hand on my back. "You trust your gut, Mel. Always have. So do we."

"It is too early to call the police." Chaz says, "They won't do anything for at least 48 hours."

Jaxon pulls me into a hug and holds me. I know I am shaking like a leaf. She is not just my best friend; she is the closest thing I have to a sister.

Brody pulls out his own phone and scrolls through his contacts, then presses a name. I already know who he's calling. Noah Ferguson. If something's really wrong, he's the one who can find her. And if something happened to Ivy? God help whoever's behind it.

Noah

I am doing rounds at The Spice Club tonight when my phone buzzes on my private line. I know it has to be someone from The Society. I keep walking and answer.

"Ferguson."

"Noah," Brody's voice is sharp. Urgent. "We need a favor."

I get to the security office, and walk in as I ask, "What kind of favor?"

"It's Ivy."

"What about her?" I ask flatly.

"She's missing."

I pause. "Define 'missing.'"

"She landed an hour and a half ago. She was supposed to come to the house after dropping off her things at her house, but never showed. She's not answering her phone. Her location's off. And the airport confirmed her flight arrived, and she went through customs."

I sit back slowly. "That's not good."

"No, it's not." Brody's voice drops, turning darker. "She doesn't just disappear, Noah. Her phone is always on, and she and Melody always share their locations."

I pinch the bridge of my nose. This isn't exactly the kind of shit I normally do. I don't do missing persons. The work I do at Elite Security is clean, professional. It is VIP protection, risk assessments, and quiet removals when someone threatens our events. I don't chase down models who forget to charge their phones.

"Look," I say, dragging a hand down my face. "She's high-profile. Has friends in the right places. I'm sure local law enforcement can handle—"

"Come on, man." Brody cuts me off. "You know the cops won't do a damn thing until it's been forty-eight hours. We don't have that kind of time."

He's right. I hate that he's right. Still, I hesitate. My instincts are warning me this is a rabbit hole. And when I go in, I don't come back out clean.

"What's the last confirmed sighting?"

"The airport," he answers. "Flight 4436. Landed at 9:17 PM. Melody tried everything, calls, texts, and even her tracking app. Nothing and not a word from her since the plane taxied the runway."

I stare at the screen in front of me, watching the empty hallway of the club flicker in static. Something gnaws at the back of my mind, low and persistent. A name like Ivy Baldwin brings attention. Kidnapping her wouldn't be random. It would be strategic. But no one's been called for ransom, and no public statement of demands has been made, but it is still early to tell. But it could also mean that it is personal.

"Fine," I say finally. "Send me her flight info, full name, a photo, the time of arrival, basically everything you've got."

Relief washes through Brody's voice. "You'll take it?"

"I'll look into it. That's not the same thing."

"Close enough for me." He exhales hard. "We're all here at the house. Melody is freaking out, man. You find her and you'll be saving more than one life."

I end the call and toss my phone onto the desk. Damn it, just what I need.

Noah

Ten minutes later, I've got her itinerary on my screen. Ivy Baldwin. First class. Delta. Landed at 9:17 PM, terminal C6.

She should've walked straight from customs to the pick-up area. Standard. Security cameras would've caught her. If she got into a car, there'd be plate footage. But I'm not trusting airport footage alone. I want eyes. My own.

I tap into a private back channel, one of our surveillance partnerships with transportation networks. Within moments, I have access to the terminal's exterior cams. I scroll until I see her. I freeze the frame, and there she is stepping through the sliding doors just before 9:50 PM. Alone. Wearing a dark green trench, sunglasses perched high despite the hour. She's dragging a signature LV roller behind her, posture perfect, every step smooth. Typical Ivy.

Then a taxi pulls up. It looks clean. The driver gets out. Opens the door for her. I zoom in on his face. He's wearing sunglasses... at night. Now, that looks suspicious all on its own. I fast-forward a few seconds, then I see her hesitate before she gets in, and the car pulls off. I freeze the frame again to get a look at the license plate to start a trace. It comes back as unregistered, which means the plate is probably stolen from a dealership somewhere. My pulse ticks up. This wasn't opportunistic. This was planned.

I open a second channel, call up the DMV cross-reference program, and enter the make and model. Bingo. The real plate number was reported stolen yesterday from a dealership three cities away.

Damn it. I slide my chair back and call Brody and tell him what I have found so far, and assure him that I will get a team of my guys working on it.

I leave The Spice Club and let my head security guy there know that I am gone for the night. I head to my office downtown, and on the way, I call in five of my staff to meet me there. When Andre, Shawn, Joey, Al, and Kurt show up, I tell them what is going on.

"First, we need all traffic cameras flagged along the route out of the airport, looking for this red Ford Crown Vic. Custom tint. Al, call your contact at the police station and tell them the cameras we need access to. Once they give you access, you and Kurt look through them and find me what exit it took."

"You got it, Boss."

"Andre, get online and find out everything you can on Ivy."

"Shawn, find out how her agent is and give them a call. Find out if she has had any threatening calls or mail."

"Joey, head over to the airport and see if you can find out anything from there. I am going to talk to Melody and see if she has any idea who could have taken her.

As they scramble, I get up and start to head out the door to speak with the guys and Melody. As I am driving, I ponder some questions. Who would go after Ivy Baldwin? A stalker? A bitter ex?

My phone pings a text message from Al.

CAMERA HIT: Intersection 12th and Broad. Vehicle spotted at 10:06 PM. Turned east. But that's where we lost them.

Shit. I type back: Keep looking. It has to show back up somewhere.

Chapter Four
On the Hunt

NOAH

THE HOUSE IS LIT like a beacon when I pull up; every damn light in the house is on. I cut off the engine. My boots crunch over the stone path leading to the front door. I don't knock. Brody already texted that it's open. I step inside, close, and lock the door behind me.

I can feel the tension and heaviness in the air. I walk into the living room, and no one's speaking. I find Melody on the couch between Jaxon and Brody. Chaz is pacing near the fireplace, jaw clenched, arms folded so tight across his chest I can see the veins in his forearms from here. Melody's eyes snap up to mine. I see the panic and desperate hope in them that I'm walking in here with good news. I wish I were.

"Noah," Brody says, rising from the couch. "What've you got?"

I nod once, walk toward the center of the room, and take out my tablet. I swipe to the relevant feed, pulling up a still frame of the car Ivy got into. It's grainy, but it's clear enough, a red Crown Vic, blacked-out windows, the plate number half-visible before it turns a corner.

"Airport cameras caught her leaving in this vehicle at 9:50 PM," I say. "A traffic camera caught sight of the car at the Intersection of 12th and Broad at 10:06 PM. Due to the tinted windows, we can't see anyone inside the car. At the airport, the driver wore sunglasses."

Jaxon leans forward; his eyes locked on the screen. "That's eastbound."

"Yeah," I say, zooming in and tapping the timestamp. "They turned east onto Broad, and then... nothing. That area's a surveillance dead zone. Half those blocks haven't had working city cameras since 2016."

"You're telling me that's where they vanished?" Chaz asks, voice low and lethal.

I nod. "That's where we lost them."

They all sit quietly. Melody closes her eyes and presses a hand to her chest, like she's holding herself together with sheer will. Jaxon sets a hand on her knee, grounding her.

"I have two of my guys sweeping the surrounding blocks now," I continue. "If she's still in that area, we'll find her."

"If?" Melody echoes, her voice cracked glass.

I turn to her slowly. "I'm going to find her."

Her lips tremble slightly, but she nods.

I take a slow breath and lower the tablet. "I need your help, Melody."

She looks up, startled.

"I need to know if Ivy's had any problems lately, any threats, or obsessive fans. Exes who didn't take no for an answer. Anything that might point to someone targeting her intentionally."

Melody blinks, and I can see the thoughts racing behind her eyes.

"She doesn't really get any of that information. Her agent gets all her mail and usually handles anything that needs to be handled," she says finally. "But..."

"But what?"

"There was a guy," she says, sitting up straighter now. "About a year ago. After her contract ended with her last Dom, Paul. She mentioned someone following her after a shoot in Milan. He didn't approach her, but he showed up again in New York a few weeks later. Same guy, but she brushed it off as a coincidence."

"Did she report it?" I ask.

She shakes her head. "No. She laughed it off. Said it was probably someone from the crew who just happened to be traveling. But... she was lying. I know her. She was scared."

I pace a few steps. "Did she give you a name? A description?"

Melody bites her lip. "No. But she said he was small. Average height. White. Very clean-cut. The kind of guy you'd never look at twice."

That tracks. Perfect profile for someone hired to snatch a high-value target.

"Anyone else?" I press.

Melody shakes her head. "Not that I know of. She ended things with Paul on her own. It broke her, but he didn't pursue her after. He wasn't that kind of Dom. Cold, sure, but not cruel."

"I think Ivy was targeted specifically. She is famous enough to draw headlines if she vanishes, but private enough that she doesn't have a swarm of bodyguards around her 24/7. It makes her a vulnerable target without looking like one."

"So now we wait?" Melody asks, her voice paper-thin.

"No," I say. "Now I dig. Deeper than the cops. Faster than the press. And with less mercy than either."

I walk over to her and crouch down so we're eye-level. "I need anything Ivy might've left behind. Notes. Emails. Old text threads. Even things that felt insignificant. If she mentioned a weird car, a wrong number, a gut feeling, anything, I need it now."

She nods slowly. "Okay."

"Good," I say, standing again. "Because someone made a mistake tonight."

"What mistake?" Brody asks.

"They snatched the wrong person. I doubt they know anything about The Society, and how well-connected we are."

My phone rings just as I'm closing their front door. It's Shawn. The second I see his name flash on the screen, something shifts in my gut.

"Talk to me," I answer, already halfway to the SUV.

"We found the car," Shawn says, breath sharp with adrenaline. "Red Crown Vic. Parked behind a row of old warehouses off Broad Street. No camera coverage back here to see if they went into any of the buildings."

"Anyone inside the car?"

"No. Windows are blacked out, but we checked. Empty. No blood. No personal belongings. Just the vehicle. But Noah, there is something about the air back here. It's wrong."

My grip tightens on the steering wheel. "Hold position. I'm ten minutes out."

I floor it. The industrial section of Broad Street is a ghost town. There are dozens of warehouses long abandoned or half-condemned. The silence is thick, disturbed only by the low rumble of my tires and the pulse of adrenaline in my neck. When I reach the end of the street, I see the car parked at an angle behind a rusted-out fence. Shawn waves me over from the shadows. Al is beside him, rifle strapped to his chest, expression grim.

"Vehicle's cold," Shawn mutters. "We gave it another look. Not a damn trace inside. No prints, no blood. Whoever drove her here was careful."

I nod. "Which warehouse is closest?"

Shawn gestures with his chin. "That one. Left side. The door's chained but loose. No signs of movement. The second one down has more drag marks in the dust, like someone walked something heavy through the entry."

I unsling the flashlight from my belt and flick it on. "We start with the first, quietly, and then if nothing, we move to the second." They both nod their heads in agreement.

The door creaks like a dying animal when we pry it open. Inside, it smells like rust, mold, and time. Dust coats everything. The air is stale. There are empty crates and a broken conveyor belt that probably hasn't run since the Clinton administration. We sweep left to right, clearing every room. There is nothing, not even a sound. She's not here.

My jaw tightens. "On to the next."

Chapter Five
Warehouse Two

NOAH

WE JOG OVER TO the next building, and the moment I step inside, my instincts go taut. It has the subtle scent of old motor oil. Then I hear a faint thump. Al notices it too. He shifts position slightly, silent and coiled.

"Back office," Shawn whispers.

I nod once. We move in formation, tight and fluid, weapons drawn but low. Just in case. As we near the back, I hear a muffled sound. Like breathing through fabric, a faint whimper. It's Ivy, I know it. Hell, I feel it as crazy as that sounds. I don't hesitate. I kick the door in. Inside, the light flickers overhead, casting a dim circle across the cracked concrete floor. And there, bound to a chair and gagged, is Ivy.

Her eyes snap open wide. But when she sees me, her whole body sags with relief. Then everything happens at once. There is movement from the corner, and a man steps out of the shadows with his gun raised.

I shout, "Down!"

Ivy ducks instinctively. Al doesn't hesitate and fires off two clean shots. One to his chest and the other to his shoulder. The man hits the wall, then the floor. He's dead before his body settles.

Shawn rushes to Ivy while I holster my weapon and move to untie her.

"Hey," I murmur, cutting through the ropes. "You're okay. We've got you." I pull the gag from her mouth.

Her voice is hoarse. "Took you long enough."

Despite everything, a sharp laugh breaks from my chest. "Had to be dramatic."

She blinks rapidly, shaking, but not crying, not yet, at least.

I cup her cheek. "You're safe now."

Her next words hit harder than a bullet.

"No, I'm not," she whispers. "That wasn't the man behind this."

I go still. "What?"

"He said it to me in the car when I questioned where we were going because I noticed he wasn't going the right way. He wasn't the one who wanted me. He was just paid to bring me here and wait."

My stomach sinks. "Did he say who?"

She shakes her head. "Only that 'the man in charge would come for me soon.'"

Fuck.

I stand and grab my phone, pacing a few steps as I call Brody.

He answers on the first ring. "Noah?"

"We found her," I say, eyes locked on Ivy. "She's alive. We're bringing her out now."

"Thank God," he breathes. "Is she okay?"

"Shaken. But strong." I pause. "Brody... the man who had her pulled a gun out and we shot him, thinking this was all over, we didn't think we needed to keep him alive. But he wasn't the one behind it. Ivy said he was hired. Someone else is pulling the strings."

A long silence. Then, "What do you need?"

"I need to disappear."

He's quiet for half a beat. Then, "You're taking her off the radar."

"Exactly. Until we know who the real threat is. Until I end this."

"You have what you need?"

"I know just the place."

"Is there anything we can do here to help?"

"Keep her safe," he says, voice steady.

"I will. Tell Melody not to worry. I got her, and I won't let anything happen to her."

Twelve Hours Later - The Cabin

It's just past sunrise when I pull up to my stepdad's old cabin in the middle of nowhere. It's definitely off-grid, with no smart tech or cameras. There's no electricity, only a solar rig and an emergency generator. It's been mine for years, but on paper, it doesn't officially belong to me. It's perfect for hiding her away while the team tracks down this maniac.

I kill the engine and glance at Ivy in the passenger seat. She hasn't said much since we left. She's curled beneath one of my hoodies, her eyes hidden behind sunglasses.

"I know it's not exactly five stars," I mutter. "You're used to luxury, not mosquito screens and space heaters."

She turns slowly, pushes the glasses up, and smiles.

"It's perfect," she says.

I blink. "Seriously?"

"It's quiet, simple, and looks safe out here in the middle of nowhere." She exhales. "You think I need marble floors and imported sheets to feel okay?"

"Well," I say, walking around to grab our bags, "you are a runway queen."

She steps out, stretching like a cat. "Maybe I am now. But I just don't want to have to be terrified someone is going to find me." *He really has no idea that even though I am a famous model, I still love the simple things in life.*

I watch her as she walks up the wooden steps and pushes open the door like she's done it a hundred times. I am shocked that she just embraced the little cabin in the woods instead of rejecting it like I thought she would. I always see her as this snob who cares only about limousines, mansions, and expensive bags. Could I be wrong? And if I am, that changes everything.

Chapter Six
Reflection

IVY

WHEN THE DOOR CRASHED open, I thought I was hallucinating. The hours in that warehouse had stretched into something warped and endless. My body was sore, my mind fraying, my skin crawling with the kind of fear I have never felt. But when that door flew inward and Noah Ferguson stormed in like a war god carved from darkness and rage, all I could do was stare. I was surprised he was the one looking for me, but I was also relieved it was him, someone I knew. Even though he is the same man who couldn't bother to give me the time of day at The Dungeon and who looked at me like I was nothing more than glitter and attitude. Crazier thing is that I'd never felt safer.

His touch was rough but gentle where it needed to be. His jaw was tight. His eyes swept over me like he needed to verify every inch of me was still in one piece. The moment the ropes fell away, he caught me as I fell over in relief. But there was no time to talk. In the same second he caught me, we were moving. His hand curled around mine as we fled that awful place.

And now we are at a cabin nestled deep in the woods, surrounded by pine trees and silence, except for the birds chirping. I have no idea how long we were driving. I have no idea in what direction we went. I just remember him meeting some woman along the way who gave him several bags, some of which looked like groceries, and we were off again. I felt like I was in a trance since he saved me. Like maybe it was all just a bad dream, even though I really know that it wasn't. But I stepped out of the car, and I can finally breathe.

I curl up on a leather couch that's older than I am with Noah's hoodie wrapped around me like armor. He's in the kitchen, if you can call a corner with a stovetop, an old fridge, and a French press a kitchen, pacing slowly with his phone pressed to his ear. His voice is low, calm, but there's tension in his shoulders, worry maybe. He keeps checking the windows even though he swore we weren't followed. He closes every conversation with the same quiet warning: *"Update me the second you know anything."*

I should be tired or at least processing what just happened. But I'm just numb. Like I see and hear everything going on around me, but I am just that, hearing it, and not listening to it.

He walks over, handing me a glass of water before settling into the chair across from me.

"You should sleep."

I shake my head. "Not yet."

"You haven't closed your eyes since I found you."

"I know," I whisper. "I'm afraid if I do... I'll wake up back there."

He doesn't respond right away. He just watches me with those intense eyes.

"You won't," he says finally. "I'm here now."

I don't know what to say to that. So, I just nod.

He gets up and walks to the door. "I am going to just walk around the cabin. I will be back in just a few minutes. Maggie brought us some clothes and food. I put your bag in the bedroom when we arrived. I will fry some fish when I get back. You do eat fish, don't you?"

"Yes, thank you, and for the clothes."

"She went shopping for you. They should fit. She got your size from Melody. They are not expensive, but they are what you need to wear out here."

"I do wear normal clothes, you know."

He grins, nods his head, and walks out the door.

The sun slips behind the trees sometime after eight. We haven't eaten dinner for long. The cabin is so quiet, except for the creaking of the wooden walls and the occasional chirp of insects outside. There is no Wi-Fi and no TV. There is a fireplace, a few oil lamps, and the soft crackle of Noah moving around in the other room. He gave me the only bedroom, of course. The mattress is firm. The sheets are old cotton, worn soft. I lie there, eyes wide open, staring at the ceiling for what feels like hours until I finally feel myself drifting off to sleep.

I'm back in the chair, tied to it by the same rope on the same cold floor. But this time, no one comes to rescue me. I hear footsteps circling me. Cold hands brushing my face. A voice I can't place whispering, "You thought this was over?"

I scream, but nothing comes out. My mouth opens wide, but there is no sound. Just a deep, pressing weight on my chest as if the fear itself is trying to smother me. Then I hear the gunshot, not one, but two. They echo through the warehouse. My body jerks. Something warm trickles down my back. He shot me and I am left here to die all alone.

I scream so loud that I jolt awake. The room is too dark. I fight the sheets tangled around me, heart slamming against my ribs like it wants to escape. I can't breathe. Then suddenly, I feel strong arms wrap around me.

"It's okay," Noah's voice grounds me, low and firm. "I've got you."

I don't even know how he got in here so fast. But he's here sitting on the edge of the bed, one arm around my shoulders, the other hand on the back of my neck, holding me still like I might fall apart.

I sob once, a low broken sound, and try to swallow the rest, but he doesn't let me.

"You're safe," he says again, softer now. "It was just a bad dream."

I shake my head, fists clutching his shirt. "It wasn't. It—It felt so real."

His voice drops lower. "I know."

"I thought I was back there. He—he was behind me. I couldn't breathe. He said it wasn't over."

Noah pulls me into his chest fully, lifting me from the bed like I weigh nothing. He sits down against the headboard, cradling me in his lap like I'm something precious instead of something broken.

"It's not real," he whispers into my hair. "You're not there anymore."

But the thing is...some part of me still is.

Noah doesn't rush me. He doesn't ask questions or fill the silence with platitudes. He holds me there, letting my breathing sync with his. It takes longer than I expect, longer than I want, but eventually, the world stops spinning. The panic dulls from a scream to a hum. My fingers unclench from his shirt, and my body stops trembling in his arms.

"I didn't think it would hit me like that," I murmur, still curled into him.

"It always does," he replies. "Not when you expect it. Not when you think it should. But it always does."

I pull back just far enough to see his face in the low light from the hallway. His features are sharp, jaw shadowed with stubble, eyes dark but alert. There's something different in the way he's looking at me now, something gentler than I would have ever expected from him.

"Do you have them too?" I ask.

He nods. "Not so much anymore. But yeah. I used to. After my last op overseas. Before I started Elite."

He finally shifts, gently moving me to sit beside him on the bed. I catch a flash of hesitation in his movements, like he's not sure if I want him to stay. But I do. God, I do.

"Noah?"

"Yeah?"

"Can you just... stay a little while?"

He gives me the smallest nod. "Yeah. I can."

He doesn't lie down. He leans back against the headboard and lets me curl against his side, my head on his shoulder, one of his hands resting lightly on my leg like an anchor.

I close my eyes, listening to his heartbeat. It's slow and steady. In the soft, dark hush of this quiet cabin, I drift back to sleep feeling completely safe knowing he is right there.

The Next Morning...

I wake to the smell of coffee. At first, it confuses me, and I don't remember where I am. Then, like water rushing into a waterfall, it all comes back: the kidnapping, Noah and his team rushing in, the gunshots, the dead man who was hired by someone else to take me, and the cabin far in the woods. I remind myself that I am safe.

I get out of bed and walk barefoot into the kitchen, still wearing Noah's hoodie, the sleeves rolled twice so I can use my hands. He stands by the counter in a plain black tee and grey joggers, barefoot as well, with a mug in hand.

He glances up. "Morning."

"Is it?"

He shrugs. "Technically."

He gestures toward a second mug on the counter. "It's strong. You'll thank me later."

I take it, cradling the ceramic in my hands like it might keep me standing. "Thanks... for everything."

He meets my eyes. "You don't have to thank me. You didn't deserve what happened to you."

"That's not what I meant," I say softly. "I meant for you to come for me. For not giving up."

His jaw tightens slightly, like the compliment makes him uncomfortable.

"You're Melody's best friend. I wasn't going to let anything happen to you."

We drink in silence for a while. And when I catch him looking at me, I see something new in his eyes that I hadn't seen before. Maybe he is starting to realize that I am not just who everyone sees on the runway, but I am humble and not moved by material things, even if I have them.

Chapter Seven
The Realization

NOAH

A s I HEAR THE slight click of Ivy's mug against the
kitchen counter as she pours more coffee, her hair
still a messy halo of waves from sleep, I start to think
about her reactions to being here. She went from runways
and spotlights to being kidnapped and held in a rundown
warehouse to be whisked away to a cabin hidden deep in
the woods to keep her safe. She doesn't complain about
the limited cell service or ask when she's going back to
civilization. She... settles in. I didn't expect her to be the
kind of woman who could be stripped of all the polish and
glitz and still function.

I continue to watch her from the front porch as she
walks by me barefoot into the yard. The hem of her leg-
gings soaked from the morning dew in the grass. There's
a small cluster of wildflowers blooming near the treeline,
and she crouches down to trace her fingers along the petals.
Just like that, Ivy Baldwin, runway royalty, cover girl, for-
mer submissive to a cold bastard in London, is kneeling
in the woods like she was born there. And for a moment,
I forget why we are here. Then I remember her scream.

The way it tore through the cabin last night like a blade. The way she shook in my arms afterward, breathing like she was drowning, and the air itself was the water. She hasn't mentioned it this morning. But I saw the shadows under her eyes when she stepped out of the bedroom. I saw how tightly she wrapped herself in my hoodie again, even though the day was warm. She is not okay, at least not yet. I have seen trauma before. I've lived it. And I know what it does when it sits too long in the dark without being touched. I can't fix it, but I can keep her safe until she figures out how to stand on her own again.

Later, we eat in silence: grilled cheese, soup from a can, and a couple of granola bars. Ivy doesn't complain once. She eats, slow and quiet, like her body needs the routine of it more than the food itself.

Neither of us talks much. I guess I am not sure what to say to her, and I probably have already given her the impression that night at The Dungeon that I didn't want to know her or like talking to her, for that matter. But in the last 24 hours, I have seen a different side of this woman. A side that, unfortunately, I probably wouldn't have seen if she hadn't been kidnapped. I think she is a stuck-up snob, but what does that make me? So, I decided to break the silence and have an actual conversation with her.

"We have a lot of free time on our hands. I was thinking we could get to know each other better."

"I am an open book. Ask me anything you want to know."

"Where are you from?"

"I was born and raised in Evergreen, Colorado. My parents, sister, and her family still live there."

"Evergreen, Colorado, huh? I have never heard of it."

"It is a small town in the Rocky Mountain foothills."

"And how did a girl from Evergreen make it to the famous runways of Paris?"

"I left home and headed for NYC. I have a marketing degree. While in school, I took modeling classes and went to several open calls. It wasn't quick, but once one door opened, they all flew open, and here I am today."

"Did you always want to be a model?"

"I did for as long as I can remember. And what about you? Where are you from, and how did you get into security to start Elite Security?"

"My family is from Jamaica. I guess my accent has changed a lot over the years! I served in the United States Marine Corps for twelve years. When I got out, I decided I wanted to go into business for myself and started Elite Security."

"I would say you still have a little accent left! I think it is very sexy. Twelve years is a long time. Why didn't you stay and retire?"

"Right around the time to reenlist, my mom got really sick. I decided to get out and help my sister take care of her. I started Elite Security a few months after I got out. It didn't get as big as it is now until after she passed four years ago. Then I put all my effort into it and found Mike, the owner of The Royal Grand Hotel chain, at a play party one night, and we hit it off. He got me hooked up with The Society, and the rest is history."

"How did you get into BDSM?"

"When I was stationed overseas. I was twenty-three years old and walked into a club one night and realized that I had all of these desires to be a Dom. You?"

"I was overseas as well, and it pretty much happened like it did for you. You know it wasn't something that was so openly talked about in the States then."

"No, it wasn't. And on some levels, it is still a little hidden!"

We continue to chat for a few more minutes before she decides to turn in for the night. It was in that conversation that I realized that she wasn't at all what I thought she was, and I could see myself being her Dom.

As I am lying on the couch, I hear her screams again. I know it is another nightmare. I jump up and run into the bedroom. She is still screaming and tossing the sheets around like she is fighting for her life.

"Ivy. It's me. It's Noah. I've got you. You're safe."

She opens her eyes and looks at me with so much fear. I pick her up and sit her on my lap, just like I did the night before. I pull her close to my chest and hold her until she calms down. When she does, she looks at me, and there is something in her eyes that melts me. I kiss her forehead without thinking. It was a natural reflex.

"Thank you again for coming to my rescue. I am so sorry to have woken you up."

"Don't worry about it. They will get better."

"Will you just sleep in here with me every night? I feel so safe knowing you are beside me."

I take a deep breath, "Yes, I can do that."

A few minutes later, she was sleeping, nuzzled into my side.

After eating breakfast, my phone lights up with a secure call from André. I step out the front door and onto the porch. Ivy is curled up on the couch, reading a romance novel she found on a dusty bookshelf, which must have been my mother's. But at least she looks peaceful, and right now, I need her to stay that way.

I swipe the screen and press the phone to my ear. "Ferguson."

"You alone?" André's voice is sharp, clipped, his words already wrapped in tension.

"Yes. I stepped outside on the porch," I say.

"Good. Then you can talk freely."

That sets me even more on edge. I shift to the far end of the porch, crouching next to the railing where I can watch the tree line. "What've you got?"

"We pulled Ivy's full client file from her modeling agency," André says. "Background intel. Contracts. Travel history. You were right, her schedule for the last six months was too consistent. Too public."

"I figured. She's an easy target if someone's watching patterns."

"Worse," he says. "Someone was."

I stiffen. "Who?"

"Don't know yet. But listen to this. Her agent, Clarissa Mayfield. She's been receiving mail and emails sent to the agency. Letters, dozens of them."

"Fan mail?"

"No. Threats. Obsessions. Classic stalker behavior. Most of them were cryptic phrases like 'mine soon' and 'you're wasting your time running.' Some included her photos. Others are pages ripped from fashion magazines with her eyes blacked out."

A cold rage pools low in my stomach. "And this agent… she didn't tell Ivy?"

"No," André growls. "She logged them. Marked them as 'delusional fan correspondence' and buried the reports. But she never informed Ivy or her security team. Not once."

"Jesus Christ."

"She even flagged the ones that were more… violent. But still chose to handle it internally."

"Is she in custody?"

"No, but we're building a case. At best, it's gross negligence. At worst? Conspiracy-level endangerment. Ivy had a right to know."

I rake a hand down my face, jaw tight. "You said violent. How violent?"

André sighs. "There's one message I haven't been able to stop thinking about. It came two months ago, emailed through a proxy server. Text only. One sentence: 'You won't scream when I take you, you will whimper like prey."

I feel the air leave my lungs. I think about her body trembling in my arms. Her voice, hoarse after the gag. The sound of her screaming herself awake. It was like she knew, even if she didn't see the messages, like she felt it somehow.

I stand and pace the porch, energy burning under my skin. "Have you linked it to anyone?"

"We're trying. The proxy server runs through five different countries. Whoever's behind it knows how to stay hidden. But there's a pattern—spikes in contact around her travel dates. Particularly Milan, New York, and L.A., and get this..."

"Hit me."

"One of the packages she was supposed to receive in Milan never made it to her hotel room. Security signed for it. But it vanished."

"Was it ever recovered?"

"Only the envelope. Torn open. Contents missing. No prints. No surveillance in that part of the hallway."

"That's not random."

"Exactly."

There's a pause.

Then André says, "Noah, if you hadn't tracked that vehicle, I don't know that Ivy would be alive right now."

I shut my eyes. My voice is flat when I say, "We need to figure out who it is, fast."

"We're working around the clock. But until we get something definitive..."

"I'll keep her off the radar."

There's a pause. "You okay watching her that long?"

I glance through the cabin window. She's curled on the couch, tucked beneath a quilt, her hair falling across one cheek.

"I'm not going anywhere," I say.

"Okay. I will keep you posted," André replies.

Chapter Eight
Beneath the Surface

THE LIGHT IS SOFT this morning, dappled through the trees outside the cabin windows like it's afraid to interrupt. The sky is a flat stretch of pale blue, and the air smells like pine needles and warmth and something faintly metallic from the old water heater Noah just restarted.

I'm curled on the couch under one of the woven blankets I found in the cedar chest. It's frayed at the edges, sun-bleached in places, but it smells like safety.

Noah's been outside on the porch for maybe an hour on the phone. I know it has to be with one of his guys. The moment he walked in, whatever he found out had him pissed off. I could see the steam coming from his head and the storm behind his eyes, even though he tried to shut the door gently behind him. He was so mad that it actually slammed shut. Then he stands there, eyes on me, hands flexing at his sides like he's preparing to brace me for impact.

I sit up slowly, a flutter of unease rippling through my chest. "Noah?"

He moves toward me with deliberate steps, stopping just a few feet away.

"I need to tell you something," he says, voice low. "I wasn't sure if I should do it now while I am so pissed off or tomorrow after I had time to process it, but I made a promise that I wouldn't keep things from you."

I grip the edge of the blanket. "Okay."

He exhales, then starts. André called with some news. He said that they *"pulled your full client file from your modeling agency. Background intel. Contracts. Travel history. And that your schedule for the last six months was too consistent. Too public."*

I swallow hard, a sudden chill coiling in my belly. "Someone was watching me."

He nods once. "Worse. Someone was following your patterns."

My breath catches.

He paces once, then stops, hands on his hips, head down. "André found out that your agent, Clarissa Mayfield, has been receiving mail and emails sent to the agency, dozens of them."

My lips part. "I never saw anything."

Noah lifts his gaze to mine. "Because she never gave them to you."

I feel my insides aching in agony. "What kind of letters?"

He doesn't sugarcoat it. André's exact words were, *"Not fan mail. Threats. Obsessions. Classic stalker behavior. Most of them were cryptic phrases like 'mine soon' and 'you're wasting your time running.' Some included your photos. Others were pages ripped from fashion magazines with your eyes blacked out."*

I stare at him. Frozen.

Noah's jaw flexes. "She logged them. Marked them as delusional fan correspondence. Buried the reports. Never informed you."

My stomach turns. "She...she kept them from me."

"She even flagged the violent ones. But still chose to handle it internally."

The room spins. The walls of the cabin feel like they're closing in. I blink fast, but the pressure builds behind my eyes anyway.

"Is she... in jail?"

"No," he says. "But we are building a case. Gross negligence at best. Criminal endangerment at worst. You had a right to know."

I press a shaking hand to my lips. "Jesus."

Noah sits beside me slowly, keeping his movements steady. Measured. "There's one message André can't shake. It came two months ago through a proxy server, one sentence."

I nod, barely breathing.

"'You won't scream when I take you,'" he recites, *"'you will whimper like prey.'"*

The words land like a fist in my gut. My body jerks. I gasp as tears sting my eyes and something deep, primal, lurches inside me.

"Noah..." My voice breaks. "I felt it. I knew something was wrong. In Milan... in New York... even before Paris. I felt eyes on me."

He nods. "Because someone was watching."

A sob bubbles up before I can stop it. I curl in on myself, shoulders shaking, arms tight around my chest. The fear I swallowed for weeks, maybe months, rises like a tidal wave, and this time I don't fight it. I let it crash. Noah pulls me into his arms without hesitation. He holds me the way he did that first night in the cabin. His hand cradles the back of my head, the other curled around my waist as I cry into his chest. I don't know how long I cry. But eventually, the storm quiets. My body settles.

"I should've known," I whisper. "I should've pushed harder when things didn't feel right. I trusted her."

"This wasn't your fault."

"She let someone stalk me, and I was too focused on my career to even see it."

Noah pulls back enough to look at me, his eyes fierce. "You were working and living your life. She was the one tasked with protecting you, and she failed. This is not on you."

I nod, but it still hurts. Without thinking, I lean in and kiss him, a soft kiss. I barely press my lips to his before I realize what I've done.

I start to pull back, but his hand slides to the back of my neck, eyes locked on mine, and then he kisses me. It's deep, like he's been waiting for permission and finally got it. His mouth moves over mine with intent. His fingers tangle in my hair as I press closer, gripping the front of his shirt like I need him to keep me upright. When we finally break apart, we're both breathing hard. His forehead rests against mine.

His breath brushes my lips. My heart beats in my throat. The taste of him still lingers in my mouth. I don't want to move. I want to stay right here. Noah shifts first, just slightly, but then fully pulls away. He stands, turning from me so fast I barely register the movement. He exhales sharply through his nose like he's trying to ground himself.

I blink, the cold absence of him like a slap. "Noah?"

He doesn't look at me.

Instead, he mutters, "I'll be right back," and strides toward the front door of the cabin.

The screen creaks as he pushes it open, then snaps shut behind him with a finality that hits me square in the chest. I sit there in stunned silence, the echo of our kiss still humming in my skin, my lips tingling.

The minutes start to pass, and I just sit there, not moving. The wind picks up outside, carrying the scent of moss and distant rain. A bird calls somewhere in the trees, sharp and high-pitched. My fingers curl into the blanket draped across my lap. Finally, the door opens. He steps inside slowly. He doesn't meet my eyes at first. Just closes the door behind him, then stands there, his broad frame outlined in golden twilight, jaw tight, shoulders rigid.

"I shouldn't have done that," he says quietly.

The words cut deeper than they should.

My stomach sinks. "Oh."

He rubs the back of his neck like the apology is physically painful to deliver. "I let my guard down. I crossed a line."

My throat tightens. "Noah—"

"It's not professional," he continues. "And it's not what you need right now. You've been through hell. You're still trying to process what happened. And I—" He exhales hard.

My heart fractures at the edges, but I nod slowly.

"I get it," I say. My voice is softer than I want it to be. "You don't have to explain."

"I do," he says, finally looking at me. His eyes are darker now, more guarded. "Because I don't want you to think that was about me taking advantage of you being vulnerable. It wasn't that. It was—"

He breaks off, swearing under his breath. "I don't know what it was. But it wasn't fair to you."

I sit with that for a long moment. Then I rise slowly, folding the blanket and placing it on the back of the couch before walking past him to the kitchen counter. I need something to do with my hands. I pour a glass of water and take a sip even though I'm not thirsty. Then I turn to face him.

"Do you regret it?" I ask.

His expression shifts, barely. But I see the flicker of something he tries to bury.

"No," he admits. "But that doesn't mean I should've done it."

"I'm..." I pause, searching for the right word. "Disappointed."

His shoulders relax a fraction.

"But," I continue, "don't pretend it didn't mean something. Even if we both know it can't go anywhere right now."

A beat passes.

Then he nods, once, sharply. "Okay."

Silence stretches between us again, thick with everything we're not saying.

I cross my arms. "So, what now?"

"We keep things simple," he replies. "We stay focused on keeping you safe. That's all that matters."

I want to argue. I want to tell him that being safe isn't enough. That feeling alive and wanted is just as important. But I don't.

Chapter Nine
Giving in to Temptation

NOAH

THE SHRIEK JOLTS ME from sleep. My feet are on the floor before the echo dies, heart jackhammering in my chest as I vault over the battered coffee table and slam through the bedroom door.

Ivy's scream ricochets off the pine rafters. She's entangled in the crumpled sheets. Her knees drawn up to her chest, and her arms clawing at the empty air. Her face is contorted, and her eyes are fused shut. Sweat beads on her forehead.

"IVY!" My voice barrels through the room, louder than I intend. She doesn't hear me. She's somewhere else, drowning under waves of terror.

I cross the room in two strides, floorboards shuddering under my weight. I grab for her wrists. She nearly clocks me with a wild backhand, but I catch the flailing fist and twist, gently, trapping her arm across her chest. She continues to scream repeatedly.

"Easy, easy, I've got you." I slide onto the mattress and wedge my hip against her thigh to pin her down. She's all frantic motion, no sense, no direction. I can feel every muscle in her body locked and vibrating. Another scream tries to claw its way out of her, but now it's muffled.

She starts to weep. Not the beautiful, picturesque tears you see on runways, but guttural, shaking, full-body convulsions that shake the whole bed frame.

"Ivy, listen. You're safe. You're in the cabin. I'm here. I'm not leaving."

I can feel the way she tries to process my words. Her jaw flexes, her whole body shudders, but she doesn't pull away. Her hands curl into fists, then slowly uncurl, fingers splayed against my forearm. Her breathing evens, little by little. I can feel the adrenaline in her veins, the residual violence that still needs somewhere to go. She trembles less.

I glance up at the battered clock on the far wall, 03:13. My own eyelids itch with exhaustion, but I don't dare move, not until I'm sure the nightmare is over.

"Ivy," I murmur, low and close to her ear. "Look at me."

She does, finally. Her eyes crack open, white rimmed with red, pupils blown wide. The raw fear still bleeds through, but there's recognition, a flicker of relief, as if the sight of me is the only proof she's awake. She blinks hard, lashes stuck together with tears.

"Fuck," she whispers, her voice gone raw. "I can't—"

"I know," I say, tightening my hold just enough to make her feel it. "You're here. You're okay."

She goes boneless then, every muscle sagging at once. Her head lolls back onto my shoulder, damp hair smearing my t-shirt. She clings to me like a lifeline. I stroke her hair, slow and deliberate, sweeping it away from her eyes and tracing the curve of her scalp. Her breath flutters, catches, then steadies out. She turns her face into my chest, hiding from the world, and I cradle her there, letting my own heart slow to match hers. I hold her until the shaking recedes. Even then, I keep one arm locked around her ribcage, the other cradling the back of her skull.

She breathes in short, shuddering bursts, mouth open against my chest. I rest my chin on the crown of her head and stare into the dark, counting her inhales, waiting for her to speak. Instead, she shifts her cheek pressing harder into my sternum, then the slow uncurl of her fist from my arm. She flexes her fingers, then slides her palm along my forearm.

"Take it away," she whispers.

She doesn't have to say what. I see the shape of it in her face: the panic. I know what it means to want your mind emptied, to need someone else to take the wheel. I slide my fingers under her jaw and lift her chin. She watches me. I drag my thumb across her lower lip, then lean in slowly and deliberately, until our mouths meet. She makes a low noise, not a whimper, but a sound buried deep. I catch her mouth with mine, slow and unhurried, and she opens for me, as if she's been holding her breath for days. Her tongue is soft, searching, her kiss tinged with desperation. I deepen the kiss. Her body melts into mine, every ounce of struggle draining out and leaving behind pure, raw want. I shift us so she's flat on her back, head pressed into the pillow, my thigh bracketing her hips, and one hand pinning her shoulder. The sheet falls away, exposing her bare legs, the simple black underwear, and the oversized t-shirt clinging to her curves. I let go of her shoulder and run my palm down her arm, slow enough to memorize every bump of bone. I tug at the hem of her shirt, and she arches her back, wordlessly inviting me to strip her. I oblige, rolling the cotton up over her ribs, then up, over her head. As the shirt passes her eyes, I let it linger, bunching the fabric around her forehead using it as a blindfold. Her body goes rigid again from the sudden absence of sight, the anticipation, the gasp of adrenaline as she surrenders her world to me. I knot the sleeves behind her head, gentle but unyielding, and her lips part in a soft moan.

"Is that what you want?" My voice is low, roughened by need.

"Yes," she breathes, and there's not a molecule of doubt in it.

I let my hands map her, down the line of her neck, the strong curve of her clavicle, the gentle slope of her breasts. I pause, watching the way her chest rises and falls, every breath visible in the moon's silver. Her nipples tighten under my fingers, dark and hard, and she shudders when I roll one between thumb and knuckle.

I kiss my way down her throat, slow, relentless, until she's gasping. I press my mouth to the hollow just above her heart, and she makes a sound that's half-sob, half-laugh. I drag my hand lower, over her stomach, along the sharp edge of her hip bone.

She tries to rise up, to guide my hand, but I clamp her wrist back against the mattress and wait. "Don't move," I say, and she freezes, instantly obedient.

I leave her waiting, hovering above her, and watch her for a moment. She is utterly exposed: hair wild and damp, arms stretched over her head, the fine tremor of her legs as she tries not to squirm. I could break her with a word, but I don't. Instead, I savor the control, the trust, the need. I trail my fingers up her thigh, featherlight, until I reach the cotton edge of her panties. She is already wet, the fabric dark where it touches her. I let my thumb press, gently, then draw lazy circles until she's panting, hips grinding helplessly against my hand.

"Please," she whispers, so soft I almost miss it.

I reward her by slipping a single finger under the waistband and stroking her, slow and shallow. Her whole body arches off the bed; she clings to the headboard with her free hand, knuckles white.

"Shh," I murmur into her ear. "Let me."

She does. She lets go, entirely. Every moan, every gasp, every twitch is a message written on skin for me to read.

I take my time, building her up until she's begging, voice wrecked and needy. I watch her come apart, the way her legs kick at the air, the way her lips form my name like it's the only word she remembers. When I finally push her over, it's like watching a dam burst, her whole body shaking, mouth open in a wordless scream that's all pleasure, no fear. I don't let her go, even when the aftershocks have wrung her out and left her boneless. I peel the blindfold from her eyes, kissing her brow, her cheeks, the salt on her lips.

She pulls me down, burying her face in the hollow of my neck, arms locked around me like she's afraid I'll vanish if she lets go. I hold her tight, rocking her gently, feeling her heartbeat echo against my own. We lie together; the bed sheets twisted beneath us. She sprawls across my chest, arm flung over my heart like she's staking a claim, her leg tangled around my thigh. The only sound is her slow, measured breathing, the faint click of the ceiling fan, the distant hush of wind sifting through the pines.

For a long time, neither of us moved. I just lay there staring at the ceiling. She nuzzles closer, tucks her face into the curve of my neck, and lets out a soft, contented sigh. Eventually, her breathing deepens, and she goes limp in my arms.

Chapter Ten
The Aftermath

I WAKE WITH MY cheek pressed to a solid shoulder, the sheets yanked up to my collarbones, but it's Noah's arm, heavy and unyielding, that pins me down. I can feel the night's leftover sweat clinging to my thighs, cooling in the dawn. The rest of me is blanketed in heat from his body. For a minute, I just listen to the cadence of his breath. It's steady, almost meditative, like the slow pull of tide over sand. His chest expands against my ribcage, then contracts, his pulse ticking off time under my palm where it's mapped to the flat of his sternum. I move my hand half an inch just to prove I can, fingers grazing the sharp rise of his collarbone, and he doesn't react. No twitch, no military micro-flinch. Out cold. I almost laugh. His face, seen sideways and a little out of focus, is less intimidating than usual. Mouth slack, lashes dark, and the stubble at his jaw has grown overnight.

I could stay like this, but the itch to move wins out. Carefully, I inch my way out from under his arm. His fingers twitch in protest, but I shush him with a soft touch at the back of his hand. He lets go. I sit up, sheets slip down to my hips, and the air knifes across my bare skin. Every nerve wakes up at once, and I curse under my breath. The memory of what happened here last night hangs in the air, sticky and unshakeable, but I try not to think about it too hard. I have no idea what is going to happen today when he wakes up. *Will he apologize? Will we pretend like it didn't happen and not mention it at all?*

I put back on the t-shirt I had last night and stand up. As my feet hit the floor, it is freezing. I let out a little shiver noise from the bottom of my throat and hope I don't wake him. There's a thin seam of light bleeding through the slit in the curtains, and I follow it to the window. I move the edge of the curtain and peer outside. I see a deer just barely at the tree line, just standing there. I watch the world brighten for a few minutes, the slow reveal of sun on the needles, the haze above the mossy clearing. In the city, dawn always means an onslaught of cars, sirens, the endless click of camera shutters, and strangers staring at your face like it's for sale. Out here, nobody is looking. I try to imagine myself living this way: up with the sun, no schedule but my own, nothing to do but breathe and exist and let the day start clean. I can't picture it as a full-time life, but to be able to get away from the hustle and bustle and come here to refresh, I can definitely see that.

Behind me, Noah stirs. The mattress dips, the covers rustle. He doesn't say anything, but I can feel his attention snap awake. I leave the window, cross the room, and perch on the edge of the mattress. His eyes are still closed, but I know he's not asleep. His breathing has changed, like he is waiting for me to make the next move. I reach out and touch his face, thumb tracing the line of his cheekbone.

I lean in and, before I can overthink it, kiss the spot just below his temple, a breath of pressure and nothing more.

His eyes open, slow and heavy-lidded, pupils wide in the thin morning light. For a second, he looks at me like he's assessing a threat, or maybe just trying to translate what happened last night. I half expect a quip, a command, some snarky deflection. He sits up, slow and deliberate, like every joint needs time to check in before it'll cooperate. He's shirtless, wearing only the dark boxer briefs he'd tugged on half-awake. The muscles in his chest and stomach flex as he stretches, a ripple of authority even in something as simple as a yawn. He props himself against the headboard and lets his head fall back, neck exposed, eyes closed for a second, before he lifts one hand to the back of my neck and pulls me down onto the bed beside him. I go willingly.

His eyes pin me, all dark and calculating. "How do you want this to end?"

I laugh. It comes out wrong, too brittle. "With both of us alive. That'd be a start."

He smiles. "Well, I think that is a given, but let me rephrase: where do you want this to go?"

In a nervous voice, I tell him, "Well, when Brody first introduced us, I wasn't looking for a new Dom, a relationship, nothing. When you came at me with the snobby, famous model shit, I decided that I would come back from Paris and prove to you that I was more than a famous runway model. This morning, I don't want to play games, I don't want to go toe-to-toe. I hope you see the real me."

"Well, I do see the real you now, and when all of this is over," he says, low and calm, "I want to be your new Dom." The words hang there, suspended between us.

"Not because you need one. Because I want it. And I think you do, too."

It feels like stepping out onto a glass bridge. Every cell in my body says run. But his hand is at my back, and I'm tired, so fucking tired, of pretending I don't care about being kept.

"I do," I say, voice so small it barely registers.

He lifts my chin with two fingers, and for the first time, his eyes aren't evaluating, or guarding, or expecting me to fail. They're just open. "I'm not going to be gentle with you, Ivy. That's not what you need."

My breath hitches. I nod once, sharp and confident.

"I care about you," he says, as if confessing to a war crime. "More than I ever expected to."

I reach up and cover his hand with mine, tracing the lines of his knuckles, then thread my fingers through his. My palm is dwarfed by his, but I hold tight.

"You're a lot to handle," I say, voice rough with morning.

"You can handle it." He kisses me not hard or possessively, just... claiming.

I know there is a lot more to talk about with him becoming my Dom, but right now, I know we have to focus on what is right in front of us, me being safe, and my stalker being caught.

I get up and go take a shower while Noah goes into the kitchen. The water is hotter than it probably should be.

It hits my shoulders in long, steady streams, unraveling the knots in my neck as steam swirls around the small bathroom like mist curling off a lake. I brace my hands against the cool tile and let my head hang forward, breathing deeply. I turn the dial slightly hotter. The water runs over the curve of my back, trails down my thighs. I close my eyes and let it massage my body from the amazing night of sex we just had. I can't wait for him to be my Dom.

When I finally step out, I wrap myself in the oversized towel. My cheeks are flushed. My eyes were still shadowed with exhaustion. But I look more like me than I have in weeks. The thought makes something tight in my chest loosen, just a little.

After I wrap myself in the towel, I follow the scent of bacon into the kitchen. Noah stands at the stove in a plain black T-shirt and dark jeans, barefoot, spatula in hand. The way his shirt pulls across his shoulders makes my mouth go dry. He hears me and glances back. His eyes sweep down my towel-wrapped frame, then snap up again, and he clears his throat.

"Hope you're hungry," he says, turning his attention back to the sizzling pan.

I smile faintly, walking to the counter. "What, no croissants? No room service?"

He snorts. "This is the Ferguson Special. Bacon. Eggs. Toast. If you want a mimosa, there's orange juice and... well, orange juice."

I slide onto one of the stools. "Honestly? This is better than anything I've had in days."

He plates the food with practiced ease, hands it to me, then grabs his own and sits across from me at the narrow kitchen table. We eat in comfortable silence for a while, the kind that's almost startling in how easy it feels.

Eventually, he leans back in his chair and stretches. "Is there any hot water left?"

"I left you some," I tease, standing and collecting our plates. "But only because you fed me."

"Well, I figured that was the least I could do after wearing you out last night! But the way you came out of that shower in nothing but a towel gives the impression that you haven't had enough yet!"

"I was starving, and it smelled so good. But I will always be ready when you want me to be!"

"That is good to know. I am glad to hear that for future reference." And he gets up to head to the shower.

I giggle.

I rinse the dishes, glancing over my shoulder more than once, even though I can still hear the rush of water behind the bathroom door. My pulse picks up anyway when I hear him turn off the water, wondering if he will be ready for another round.

He steps out a few minutes later, towel slung around his neck, in just a pair of sweatpants, and damn, he looks edible. I open my mouth to say something, maybe joke about the fog still following him out of the bathroom, but his phone buzzes sharply on the table and cuts through the morning calm.

He glances at the screen, then picks it up. "It's André."

I freeze.

His eyes flick to mine. "Stay close."

He answers the call and walks to the window, phone pressed to his ear.

"Yeah?" A pause. "You sure?" Another pause. His entire body stills. "You found him."

The silence that follows is heavy—my heart stutters. Noah turns slowly, eyes locked on mine now.

"I'll keep her here. Text me everything."

He ends the call.

My breath hitches. "Noah...?"

He crosses to me in three long strides, voice low, steady, but not calm. "They know who it is. The team is on its way to get him. André will call me back in a few minutes."

Chapter Eleven
The Takedown

ANDRÉ

I**T'S JUST PAST MIDNIGHT** when the alert hits my phone. Not a ping. Not a buzz. A full-blown override on the encrypted server we've been running in the background since the night Ivy Baldwin vanished. The facial recognition software finally hits a solid match.

Randall Pierce.

Location: Warehouse District. Westside. Building C.

The adrenaline hits before I even finish scanning the profile. Everything in me goes cold and locked, like a combat-mode autopilot takes over. I hit the call button for Noah. He answers on the first ring. His voice is all gravel and restraint.

"Tell me you've got something."

"Yeah. We got him." My voice stays even. Sharp. "Randall Pierce. Freelance data analyst. Shell companies across three states. The IP address was used to send four of the stalker emails. Security footage confirms he entered Ivy's last hotel in Milan. Warehouse on Broad Street matches his rental. He's there now."

"I want to be on the phone the whole time," Noah growls. "Step by step. I want to hear him taken down."

"You got it." I click my earpiece into place, grab my Glock and vest, and send the green light to Tray, Kurt, and Al. Tonight, we end this for our Noah and Ivy so they can both come home.

The SUV hums beneath me as I cut through the sleeping city, tires slicing damp asphalt. The warehouse looms ahead. It has rusted metal sides and half the letters on the signage eaten by time. Tray is crouched behind a dumpster when I arrive. He gives me the signal that there is movement inside. Al's got overwatch on the rooftop, Kurt is already circling from the back. I press my earpiece.

"Noah. You with me?"

"Yeah. I've got you. Let's bring him in."

I draw my sidearm, nod to Tray, and we move. Quiet. Coordinated. Like muscle memory.

Tray picks the side door's lock and eases it open. Inside, the warehouse is dark, except for a flickering light swinging over a desk littered with monitors. I scan the space. That's when I see him, Randall Pierce.

Mid-thirties. Dirty blond hair, pale and thin. He's hunched over one of the monitors, staring at Ivy's face frozen on a paused video still. He is muttering something I can't make out.

"Randall Pierce," I say, voice loud and firm. "Hands in the air. Now."

He jolts, but instead of panicking, he slowly turns and stares at me. Then he smiles.

"She sent you?" he says. His voice is quiet and calm. "I knew she'd be careful."

"Hands."

He lifts them. Tray cuffs him, and I keep my weapon trained until he's secured.

We sweep the room. There are flash drives, hard drives, shelves of notebooks and photos, all of Ivy. Every inch of the place is covered in her.

"We've got him," I say into the comm. "No resistance."

"I want his confession," Noah says. "Don't let him clam up."

"He won't."

The ride to the precinct is quiet. Randall hums, low and tuneless like a lullaby that never ends. He doesn't ask where we're going. Doesn't even blink when the cuffs tighten. I have seen sick before. But this? This is something else. We walk him into the precinct. I wave Captain Mendez over. The Elite and the police have a great working relationship, and it helps that Captain Mendez is in The Society.

"He's all yours," I tell her. "But I want to sit in."

She eyes me, then nods. "Ten minutes. You cross a line; I pull you out."

"Fair."

They bring Randall into Interrogation Two. He sits like he's waiting for tea service. Hands folded neatly on the table. That same eerie smile curling at the corners of his mouth. Mendez opens the file.

"Mr. Pierce, you're being held on suspicion of stalking, attempted kidnapping, and cyber harassment. You have the right to remain silent—"

"Why would I stay silent?" he interrupts. "I've been trying to talk to her for months."

He leans forward, eyes bright.

"You want to know why I picked Ivy?"

"Go ahead," I say coldly.

He fixes his eyes on me like I'm the only person in the room.

"Because she's perfect," he says, almost reverent. "She's the only person who looks like that and still carries sadness in her eyes. It's like she sees people the way I do. I've followed her for years. Not in a creepy way. I mean, just enough to know where she goes. Milan, Paris, Toronto, LA..."

"That is a creepy way," Mendez snaps.

He ignores her. Keeps talking to me.

"But something changed. She started pulling back, not smiling in interviews. Hiding. I knew it had to be someone, some handler or a Dom or whatever you people call them. Controlling her. Caging her. That's not how it was supposed to be. She needed me."

I keep my hands on the table, though every nerve in my body is screaming to punch the look off his face.

"And that's when you started the letters?"

He nods. "At first, just to let her know I was close. Then I got frustrated. She didn't respond. She let them keep her away. I just wanted to bring her back. Wake her up."

Mendez flips a photo from the case file, one of the threats, with her eyes blacked out.

"You sent this?"

Randall shrugs. "That one was... a message. Like, symbolic. The others were worse. You didn't get those?"

"Explain," I say.

He smiles wider.

"The Milan hotel package? That had a necklace, one of hers. I bought it at auction and re-sent it with a note. She was supposed to find it. She didn't. It disappeared."

"It was intercepted," I say. "That was your trigger?"

His eyes flicker. "I had to accelerate the plan. That's when I hired a driver to get her. Just to talk. Not to hurt her. Just to show her."

"You think kidnapping her would have earned her trust?"

"I'm not a monster!" he shouts suddenly, fists banging the table. "She was in danger! I was trying to save her before someone else got to her!"

I stand.

"You're done."

He pants quietly, smiling again like he's proud.

"She's going to know, you know? She's going to know it was me who cared the most."

I step into the hallway and call Noah.

"He confessed," I say. My voice sounds too calm. "Stalker delusion. Worship. Jealousy. He blamed it on that old Dom of hers. Said he's been watching her for years. He said he knew that man wasn't good for her."

There's silence on the line. Then Noah's voice, low and dangerous: he better be glad you found him, and I was here with her. If I'd been the one to find him, he wouldn't be breathing now.

Chapter Twelve
Coming Home

IVY

NOAH SETS HIS PHONE on the table and walks slowly toward me. He doesn't say anything at first. My breath catches. André said they knew who the stalker was, but did they catch him?

"Noah?" I whisper.

He exhales through his nose and crouches in front of me. "They got him."

It takes a second for the words to register. I let out a long breath and put my hands over my face, and leaned into them.

"Randall Pierce," he says. "That's his name. The one who's been sending the messages. The one who had you taken. He's in custody."

I feel my body go weightless. He sees the change in me and presses a hand over mine. "It's over, Ivy. He confessed. The team moved in and took him quietly. He admitted to everything at the police station. Captain Mendez took his statement. He became obsessed with you, following you around the world, hiring the man who grabbed you."

I try to speak, but I can't. My throat burns. My mind spins.

"He said... he thought he was protecting you," Noah continues, quieter now. "That he believed you belonged to him."

Tears sting my eyes. I didn't expect this moment to feel like this. I thought I'd jump up and celebrate. I thought it would feel like freedom. But instead, it feels... heavy. Like my soul finally exhaled after holding its breath for too long.

"Is he going to prison?" I ask, barely above a whisper.

"Eventually. For now, they're holding him. There's a case being built—cyberstalking, conspiracy to kidnap, failure to report threats. Your agent's under investigation, too."

"Clarissa." I grit my teeth. "Because she let it happen. Because she knew about the threats."

He nods. "Yes."

Noah reaches up, brushing a thumb gently across my cheekbone.

"You're safe now," he says.

I lean forward and hug him. His arms close around me without hesitation.

The drive to Melody's house is quiet. Noah drives with one hand on the wheel, the other resting lightly on his thigh. His eyes are focused, alert, constantly scanning. I don't think he knows how to relax. We turn onto Melody's street just as the sun breaks over the rooftops. I see the porch light still on. And then I see the front door burst open. And Melody bolts down the steps barefoot, hair wild, wearing one of Jaxon's oversized hoodies that swallows her frame.

I don't wait for the car to come to a complete stop. I throw open the door and run. We meet in the middle of the driveway. Her arms wrap around me, and we both break down at once.

"I was so worried about you," she whispers, pulling back to cup my face. "You have no idea, no fucking idea, what these days have been like without you."

"I'm okay," I say through a choked breath. "I'm here. I'm okay."

"No," she says fiercely. "You're not okay. But you're alive. And you're coming home."

Behind her, I see Jaxon, Chaz, and Brody standing on the porch. All three of them look like they've been dragged through hell. I haven't seen any of them cry before. But right now? Their eyes are glassy. Melody takes my hand and pulls me toward the porch. Brody moves first. He steps forward and wraps me in a bear hug, lifting me off the ground.

"We were all scared as hell, Baldwin," he mutters against my hair.

"I didn't exactly have a choice," I murmur with a teary laugh.

Jaxon is next. He doesn't say a word. Just holds me with his arms strong and silent around me like a shield I forgot I needed.

Then Chaz steps forward, quieter than usual.

"Welcome home, princess," he says, brushing a thumb gently along my jaw.

I blink rapidly, willing the fresh tears to stay put. "Thanks."

Noah stays back by the SUV, watching the entire thing unfold with that same unreadable expression.

Melody finally turns and calls out to him. "You coming in, Ferguson, or are you going to lurk like Batman?"

He snorts and shakes his head. "I'll come in later."

"Suit yourself," she says, pulling me inside.

The house smells like cinnamon and sage.

The second I step in, I'm hit with the memory of laughter, late-night wine, and movie marathons on this very couch.

"I made breakfast," Melody says, tugging me into the kitchen. "It's terrible. But it's warm."

There's a pile of toast, scrambled eggs, and bacon, most of it burnt.

I smile. "It's perfect."

We eat in silence for a few minutes before the questions start. One by one, they gently ask me about what happened. I tell them as much as I can about the car, the warehouse, and the letters. About the nightmares and the fear.

"I feel like I lost pieces of myself," I admit softly.

Melody squeezes my hand. "We'll help you find them again."

Jaxon nods. "You've got an army behind you now."

"You are staying here tonight. I made up the guest room for you." Melody said like she was a mother hen. I didn't argue.

For the rest of the day, we all watched TV. They stopped asking me questions and tried to help me feel normal.

Later in the evening, Melody leads me upstairs to the guest room. Noah appears in the doorway, leaning against the frame.

"They wanted you to stay here tonight," he says.

"Yes, Melody is being her overbearing mother hen self," I say softly.

He steps inside and looks around.

I pause, "Thank you. For everything."

His eyes search mine. "You don't have to thank me, Ivy. Just... be okay. That's all I care about."

I nod, swallowing a lump in my throat.

He turns to leave but pauses at the door.

"If you need anything," he says, "I'll be parked outside. Just keeping watch."

"Always the protector," I whisper.

His lips twitch into a half-smile. "Someone has to be."

Then he's gone. I close the door and sit on the bed, soaking in the familiarity of the house, my friends, and knowing Noah is still here. I really hope they find out that Clarissa wasn't involved. I think she thought it was all a prank or at least not serious.

Chapter Thirteen
Marking the Line

NOAH

TWO WEEKS AFTER WE got back, Ivy signed her name at the bottom of the contract that changed everything. She is my Submissive. She belongs to me. It's still surreal. Because not only did I not see it coming when I met her, but even at the cabin, I tried like hell to avoid it. But now, there's no denying the way my blood sharpens when she looks at me and calls me "Sir." No ignoring the silent ache that rises in my chest when she kneels without being told. And no walking away from the woman who made submission look like surrender and survival all in one breath.

Clarissa's name has been cleared. The last loose thread of tension tied to that nightmare has finally been snipped. Ivy's safe. We both are, which means it's time. Time to give her what she's been craving and what I've been denying myself. Tonight, we step into the Dungeon together for the first time, not as acquaintances, not as rescuer and rescued, but as Dom and submissive. It's time for me to take control.

The Fourth Base Dungeon hums with energy as we enter through the main corridor. Soft golden lights are casting a rich glow on the ceiling, and music vibrates low under the pulse of bodies moving around us. Doms lead their submissives by leashes, by wrists, by gaze alone. But I feel the eyes on us as we step inside. Now they know she belongs to me.

Her hand rests lightly on my arm. She's dressed in sheer black lace. It is a halter style, open down the back, the hem brushing her thighs with every step. Her collar glints silver under the lights, custom-fitted just last week. A slim tag dangles from the O-ring: *NOAH'S.* Her heels click against the marble floor as we walk past the bar, down into the main chamber. The center stage is open, and I chose it so they can watch.

I lean close and whisper into her ear, "Go to the platform and kneel. Center. Position three."

She trembles, but it's not fear. It's anticipation—the ache of waiting too long.

"Yes, Sir."

She walks ahead, head lowered, back straight, every inch of her composed in that elegant, effortless way that only Ivy has mastered. And as she kneels with her legs spread, hands behind her back, head bowed, the dungeon falls quiet.

A hush falls over the room, an almost reverent silence. Ivy kneels like a goddess cloaked in restraint. Calm. Poised. Ready. I walk slowly around her, letting the weight of the moment stretch across the room. I make no secret of my gaze, how it lingers on the delicate curve of her spine, the smooth dip of her neck, the way her fingers twitch behind her back like they crave the permission to move. I want her to feel every second of the wait.

From a small chest near the platform, I retrieve the implements I selected earlier: a soft deerskin flogger, a thin bamboo cane, silk rope, and a blindfold of midnight velvet. Nothing brutal. Nothing extreme. Just tools meant to push her, not punish her. I return to her and lean in close, letting my breath brush her ear.

"I want the world to see how you bend for me," I whisper.

"Yes, Sir."

I step in front of her, tilt her chin up with two fingers. Her eyes meet mine. I remove her lace halter, baring her breasts to the warm air and the hungry eyes circling the stage. Not a flinch. Not a flicker of shame. That's my girl. I wrap the silk rope around her torso, slowly binding her chest into a decorative harness. The rhythm is deliberate, reverent. Her breath hitches when I tighten the knots across her ribs. Her nipples peak from tension and chill. I pause, letting my knuckles graze over the bindings.

"You're stunning like this," I murmur. "Not just for me. For them, too."

She shivers but holds still.

I walk to the rack, take up the flogger, and return behind her. The first strike is light. A whisper across her back. The second is firmer. The third is sharp, precise, and claiming. She exhales, spine arching with each rhythm I set. Around us, The Dungeon murmurs. Some watch with clinical interest. Others, with desire. But all of them... all of them see her for what she is: a submissive who trusts her Dom completely. Her body sways, muscles flexing as I paint her back in soft crimson lines. Nothing too heavy. Just enough to mark the moment. I circle to face her again.

"Color?" I ask.

"Green," she whispers, voice hoarse but steady.

I drop the flogger and reach for the cane. When I tap it against her thigh, she stiffens.

"Stand. Feet shoulder-width. Hands behind your head."

She obeys, rising with the grace of a dancer. I strike once lightly across her inner thigh. Again, just above her hip. Her breath catches, but her body never leaves its position. After the sixth strike, I step close and cradle her face.

"You're breathtaking," I say.

"Thank you, Sir."

Now comes the real test. I blindfold her. Then kneel behind her, whispering instructions for a kneeling backbend. She arches, exposing her chest and belly to The Dungeon. She is open, bare, and unguarded. I kneel beside her and bite on her nipple just slightly.

"This is mine," I murmur.

She nods, lips trembling.

"This," I say louder, addressing the room, "is not the famous Ivy Baldwin. Not tonight. This is my submissive."

Applause erupts from the crowd, but Ivy doesn't flinch. She's trembling, tears slipping silently beneath the blindfold. And I know that I've broken her open, not with pain, but with trust. And that's the greatest high I've ever felt.

Ivy

The stars are out tonight. I lie curled in bed, my skin still tingling from where his hands touched, where his voice commanded, where his presence swallowed me whole. I signed that contract with full knowledge of what I was agreeing to. Submission. Service. Obedience. But no matter how many scenes we play or how deeply I fall into subspace, there's this ache in my chest that has nothing to do with kink. It's the way he looks at me when he thinks I'm not watching. It's the soft catch in his breath when he says, "Good girl". It's the way he held me after the scene at The Fourth Base Dungeon, like he didn't want to let go. Then again, maybe I am reading more into it. Even at the cabin, he never offered anything more than to be my Dom. Will he ever want more?

To Be Continued...
Keep an eye out for
The Powerful & Kinky
Society: Elite Security
Series

Masquerade Party
Also by Ireland Lorelei

Michael Anderson is the young billionaire bachelor who is the owner and CEO of *The Royal Grande Hotels and Resorts* and she's a new entry level marketing assistant in his marketing department. He's walked by her a hundred times in his offices and never really noticed her.

Abigail Baker is an average just out of college, entry level marketing associate at one of the biggest hotel and resort chains in the world. Her career goals are to work her way up the marketing chains to Chief Marketing Officer. She is focused and keeps her personal life and work life separate. Abigail meets a man at a masquerade party and unbeknown to her at the time, he is the owner and CEO of the company she she works for. She never recognized him as her CEO and of course he didn't even know she existed on his payroll. By the time she realizes who he is, they have already begun to play.

He brings out her deepest sexual desires. She wants to learn
more about the BDSM world and offers to teach her how
to be a sub, but not just any sub, his sub.
What happens when this well-established man who is fif-
teen years older than her, awakens sexual desires that she
never knew she had? Can they both keep their personal
life and business separate? Can they keep their growing
feelings for each other at bay and stick to the contract?

The Spice Club
Also by Ireland Lorelei

Allison Cramer has been in the BDSM lifestyle for almost a year. Lucas, a Billionaire and member of The Powerful & Kinky Society, is her first Dom. Eight months into the contract, Lucas starts to shows his true colors and Allison is not having fun anymore. One night he takes it too far and now she isn't sure she can continue to live the lifestyle anymore. Jason Carter, a Billionaire, owner of The Spice Club and board member of The Powerful & Kinky Society meets Allison through their mutual best friends, Mike and Abby. He wants her to be his new Sub. He asked Mike if she was contracted to anyone and Mike told her that she was. But when he finds out that it was her that The Society is protecting from Lucas and what he did to her, he becomes outraged and wants nothing more than to show this beautiful woman how a real man/Dom treats a woman/Sub. Can Jason help Allie realize that she can move forward and not all Dom's are like Lucas? In showing her how it is supposed to be, he starts to have feelings for her that he has never had before with any woman and definitely not a Sub. How does he handle these feelings?

The Fourth Base Dungeon
Also by Ireland Lorelei

Brody Carter is Jason's little brother. He followed his big brother's footsteps and joined The Powerful & Kinky Society as soon as he turned eighteen. While in college him and his frat brothers Chaz and Jaxson created Fetish Freaks, a social media platform to bring those with like kinks and fetishes together.

Chaz Rogers knew nothing about the lifestyle until he met Brody. Jaxon Santos had dabbled a little bit in the lifestyle but got heavy into it when he and Brody became best friends. When the three of them created Fetish Freaks, Chaz and Jaxon joined Brody in The Powerful & Kinky Society.

Three years after starting Fetish Freaks, the guys start a new venture that allows for the local members of the social media platform to meet and explore their kinks in a safe environment. They built The Fourth Base Dungeon. It was an open floor plan with three bars, ten beds and all the BDSM toys anyone could ask for.

On opening night of The Fourth Base Dungeon in walks actress Melody Remington. All three men are infatuated with her and decide to all try to make her their sub. They had always said that no woman would come between their friendship so sharing women was nothing new to them. The task here is will she want them all, or just one of them, or neither of them.

About Ireland

IRELAND LORELEI HAILS FROM a small coastal town in North Carolina and now calls Florida home. Her love for romance storytelling began in her teenage years, inspired by reading romance novels and watching soap operas and drama-filled movies alongside her mother.

She initially explored contemporary romance and contemporary erotica, as she found her footing as a writer. However, her true passion lies in crafting dark romance, reverse harem, and paranormal romance, all infused with a strong BDSM theme.

Beyond her writing, Ireland is a passionate advocate for social justice. Drawing from her own life experiences, she actively fights against domestic violence and racism. She is a strong voice for diversity, inclusion, LGBTQIA+ rights, and women's rights, using her platform to promote change and awareness.

https://linktr.ee/irelandlorelei